THE HAUNTING OF SHARON RECTORY

Our Truth, Our Horror
And Heartbreak

By

Emma Louise Tully

Emma Louise Tully

For my late Grandfather, Raymond McDaid.
You encouraged me throughout my writing and gave me the
knowledge behind Sharon's amazing history.
I dedicate this book to you. I am truly honoured to call you my
grandfather and I miss you every day.
1935-2020

E. L. Tully

SHARON RECTORY

DONEGAL, IRELAND

CONTENTS

ACKNOWLEDGMENTS

I have to start by thanking my wonderful family, Vincent, Lisa and Victoria for allowing me to include them in my story. They have supported me on this journey and embraced my decision to openly discuss our personal experiences living with the paranormal.

I also wish to thank my partner Gabriel. From reading early drafts, to giving me advice, you have been an amazing support system and I wouldn't have found the confidence I needed if it wasn't for you. Thank you.

I too want to extend my gratitude to Kate Houston who has helped me and my family for over twenty years in Sharon Rectory. She embraced our home and guided us through some of the most difficult times in our lives. With her help and knowledge of the paranormal, she endorsed me to write this book. Thank you for helping me make this happen.

Furthermore, I would like to thank each paranormal team that has helped us in Sharon Rectory. You have shown us not to let fear take over and helped us overcome some horrendous situations. Thank you.

A special thanks goes out to Paranormal Investigators Ireland for allowing me to discuss our findings from investigations as well as some of your personal experiences in your team.

Lastly, thanks to my publishing team who helped me make this book happen; they have done everything from editing, to creating the book's cover and assisting with marketing. Your work is greatly appreciated, and I can't thank you enough.

Introduction

Sharon Rectory is a well-known haunted house in Co. Donegal in the North-West of Ireland. Built in 1775 by Trinity College Dublin, this Georgian house took over 15 years to construct. Stone and building materials were transported by horse and cart from local quarries. Over centuries, Sharon Rectory had been owned by several families, all of which have stories to tell of their own experiences. The building is famously known for its documented double murder that took place on the 2nd of March 1797, among other deaths which occurred within the house and grounds.

My parents Vincent and Lisa Tully have spent the last 22 years restoring the house to its former glory. We as a family have experienced several encounters over the years with spirits and other unworldly entities on the property. One in particular known as 'The Blue Lady', which is thought to be the ghost of Sara Waller. Sara unfortunately was a victim of a brutal attack in her home of Sharon, which happened one stormy night in March 1797. She and Reverend William Hamilton were murdered by the United Irishmen over a vendetta against Hamilton.

The rectory once belonged to the Church of Ireland and housed Reverend Dr John Waller, his wife Sara and two nieces in their local parish of Ray. From my research Mr Waller was a fellow at Trinity College and was deemed highly valued within his field. As a respected and loving family, the Wallers brought great peace and security to their parishioners. Rev Waller was paralysed due to a horse-riding accident in his younger years and was cared for by his loving wife Sara. While the Wallers took residency at Sharon they were served by maids and butlers, who also helped Rev Waller with his everyday care. Mrs Waller was a French writer who wrote short stories and poems and dabbled in the arts. She served well within her community and helped families most in their time of need.

William Hamilton was born in December 1757 in Northern Ireland where his family had resided for nearly a century. Little is known about Hamilton's childhood but at the age of 15 he studied geology and meteorology in Trinity College Dublin, where he obtained a fellowship in 1779. A large portion of Hamilton's studies was around the Giant's Causeway in Co. Antrim but he also took an interest in observing variations of temperature and the action of rain, wind, and tide. Hamilton like most rectors at that time was also a magistrate and was very well connected within the church and state. In 1792 he penned a vigorous attack on republicanism which resulted in him being targeted for assassination. In the beginning of February 1797 there was an unsuccessful attack within his vicarage which led to Hamilton living in constant fear for his life. While he knew his political views caused dispute and his life was at risk, he employed soldiers to personally guard him for his security. Later his death would play a vital part in the Irish Rebellion of 1798, as his pro-British approach was no longer being tolerated within the Irish community.

Chapter I

I will begin my story on that fateful night in question. On the 2nd of March 1797, Reverend William Hamilton made way with his journey from Fanad to Lifford courthouse to conduct hearings for prisoners on death row. As the local magistrate he had control. He granted hangings of men, women and even children. He didn't show remorse and was classed as a cold-hearted man. After the trials, Hamilton made way alongside an armed guard from Lifford to Lough Swilly; they planned to travel by boat back to his parish as the night sky soon approached. Riding by horse and carriage, the journey usually took a few hours. They noticed the trees sway in the wind as bad weather approached. On the wet and muddy country road to port, they noticed the men standing huddled around as they glanced his course. The men shouted, "The boat isn't crossing, bad weather is approaching." At this point, Hamilton was oblivious that the United Irishmen had loomed the port's men previously that afternoon. They warned them not to let him on the boat. The men didn't question and acknowledged the request. When Hamilton couldn't continue, he realised he was a few miles from a former fellow of Trinity College, Rev John Waller who lived in Sharon Rectory. He had hoped the Waller family would welcome them to stay until morning.

The Rev John Waller, a fellow of Trinity College Dublin since 1768, was later appointed Rector of Raymochey Manorcunningham, where he resided with his wife, and niece Anne. Mr and Mrs Waller were a respected couple and were a great asset within their community. They would often dedicate their time to help and serve their parishioners, mostly in time of need. John Waller was paralysed from the waist down due to a horse-riding accident in his early years and was aided by servants in everyday tasks but also received much help from his loving wife Sara. Born and raised in France, Sara had great passion for writing poetry and dabbling in the arts. Through creative imagination, she devoted her time to her house and garden. With stunning blossoms and flourished trees off the patio doorstep, she loved to sit and take in the stunning scenery of Sharon. Inside, the house was grand. Large windows opened each room as the sunlight dawned from the north and dusk to south. Often, she would sit in her favourite room to write stories or poems. They enjoyed the simple life; surrounded by acres of healthy farming land and beautiful views of the Lough Swilly, they had everything for a fulfilled and peaceful retirement. Unfortunately, the Wallers had suffered great loss over the years. With the stillbirth of three babies, Sara longed to be a mother. She had this beautifully caring side that, of course, her husband and everyone in her community felt. She showed love to all who worked within her home. She made her servers feel like family and was greatly appreciative of their assistance with her husband.

As Hamilton made way to Sharon Rectory, he and his guard were warmly welcomed by the Wallers and they insisted that he'd stay until the weather was safe for him to continue his travels. The devoted Wallers unknowingly placed themselves in danger as they welcomed Hamilton into the sunroom parlour. They sat and engaged in conversations on their latest findings and local news from their parishes. The room offered a generous view of the Lough Swilly and medieval Burt Castle; they watched as the stormy dawn sky turned to grey. Little did they know, the United men hid in the shadows watching them from a distance, discussing their plan of action. They intended on the element of surprise once the night sky fell. They wanted him when he least expected. They had planned this moment since the day Hamilton penned a vital attack on republicanism, and with a previous failed attack, this needed to be executed.

As darkness soon fell, they showed Hamilton to his room where he would retire for the night. While he walked down the hallway, they heard an upheaval in the distance. Hamilton ran back into the sunroom parlour to look out of the window; there he saw the siege coming bold, charging towards the rectory. His doomsday had come. He realised this must have been a set-up and questioned whether the Wallers were in on it. The servants tried to act fast, barricading doors and windows with furniture they could physically move. They knew the attackers wouldn't stop until they got Hamilton's blood. The United men stood strong outside with their rifles, chanting Hamilton's name. They knew their fate was in the hands of the republicans. They would kill anyone who stood in their way to retrieve their enemy. They shot blindly through the windows, breaking the glass, shouting in for Hamilton; he knew his time had come.

While Sara stood by her husband's side terrified for their lives they backed into the corner of the room. Sara tried to shield her husband from fire with anything that came to hand. Hamilton dashed to the patio hallway and into the cellar, locking the door behind him. While the men continued to shoot through the windows, they shot a helpless Sara. The bullet grazed her shoulder. Her husband tried to guide her to the door safely. But while Sarah ran for the door, she was shot a second time, in the ear. Bloodied, she crawled to the hallway screaming for help as the servants ran to her aid. They struggled to move her among stooping from gunfire. They dragged her down the hallway and into to the kitchen where they lay her on the cold tiled floor. She was losing blood fast, as she fell in and out of consciousness. They knew she might not make it. Sara's breathing grew shallow as she cried to them to go to her husband. The servants wept by her side as she drew her last breath. Distraught, the cook ran up the hallway to Rev Waller where he continued to lay helpless. She dragged him to safety then bravely approached the men and pleaded with them to surrender their lives if they gave up Hamilton.

The cook ran to the cellar to retrieve their unwanted guest. Hamilton, when fleeing underground, hoped to escape through the tunnels that once ran below the property to the upper glebe. But he was mistaken. He had not realised what was once tunnels had been bricked up, leaving him trapped by the angry mob that surrounded the building. The brave cook grabbed Hamilton and led him to the men as they pulled him from behind the door, trembling and crying for mercy. They dragged him through the patio hallway towards the doorway.

Before he reached the threshold, Hamilton grabbed hold of the stair banister and held it for his life. The men pulled at his arms and legs, but he refused to let go. One of the men saw a blazing fire in the ballroom. He walked towards the fireplace and grabbed a poker from the stand, continuing to heat it over the hot flame while teasing Hamilton in the process. The other men continued to struggle with Hamilton, as the enraged one came with a hot poker to hold against Hamilton's hands. He snivelled and cried while he loosened his grip. They dragged him to the doorstep and threw him to the ground.

Mrs Waller's once beautiful garden was about to be the scene of a brutal end to the Reverend Hamilton. He sobbed aloud for them to spare his life, his screams echoing through the dead of night. The men laughed and spat on him like he was the scum of the earth. Hamilton bent on both knees continued to beg for them to spare his life. The United men weren't going to stop until Hamilton took his last breath. They began to beat him as he fell to the ground covering his head with his bloody, blistered hands. Hamilton screamed for help, crying out to his guard, but he was no more. The men drew blood as they ripped his flesh, slamming him to the earth repeatedly, then pulling him from man to man, limb by limb. He fought roaring amongst the men as they battered his weakened and broken body with stones.

Raising his head one last time to the night's sky, as his eye fell from its socket upon his bloodied, bruised cheek, he took in the aspects of the men who showed him no mercy. All bones broken within his severed body, the blood poured through the stone of the doorstep while the men continued to pull his corpse, throwing it against the walls of Sharon. Military men soon approached on horseback; they shouted to the siege for their victim. The proud United men pointed to their horses' feet as Hamilton's lifeless body lay in shards among the dirt. The murder was gruesome, so inhumanely ghastly that it would be embedded in the memories of the United men until their final days.

In the early hours of the 3rd the servants as well as Rev Waller, still hidden behind barricaded doors, opened them to find the bloodied parts of Hamilton's corpse scattered across the patio like an animal carcass ripped to a thousand pieces. After the devastation of the siege, Sara was laid to rest in the episcopal graveyard in Manorcunningham. A devastated John Waller continued to live in Sharon Rectory, horrified by his loving wife's murder and his dear friend's ghost. Mr Waller died two years later in Sharon Rectory with his niece Anne and her husband William Squire by his side. Rev William Hamilton left a wife and nine children and was buried in Derry City Cathedral. The stained, bloodied step that Hamilton's corpse lay upon was removed from Sharon, taken to

Trinity College Dublin. As for the United Irishmen, most fled overseas after the uprising but continued to relive the horrors of that fateful night. As the servants were tried as part of the acts for the murders, they were acquitted in court from all counts.

Over the decades Sharon was owned by several families, some who lived there for years and others for a matter of weeks. In the early 1900s before the floodgates were built the Swilly's tide would travel right up to Sharon Glebe. There was once only one entrance to the property which my great-grandfather John Henry maintained from time to time. He would travel by horse and cart and work on the road until the night grew dark. My grandfather Raymond McDaid would often talk to me about growing up in Newtowncunnningham and living closely to Sharon Rectory. He would remember his father taking him to the house to work on the lane as a young boy. He, his brothers and sisters would often get small jobs to help on the grounds or in the house.

From stories that were passed down from generation to generation, we were told of other deaths that occurred in the house. As two centuries had passed, it's not surprising that Sharon Rectory's history remains as shocking as the stories unfold. In 1938 another tragic incident occurred as yet another two deaths left their imprints within the walls of Sharon Rectory. During this time, the current owners employed a young couple to assist with general jobs on the property. It was unfortunate that the young lady became unwell late in her pregnancy and both she and her baby died within the house. With this great sadness, it was difficult for both families to move past such loss.

A Mr Tuilagi who was a retired German sailor bought Sharon a few years following this tragedy. There isn't much information I could find on Mr Tuilagi, but it's known that when he moved to Ireland he found and fell in love with the old rectory. When he bought the property, he changed the authentic look to the front of the house. He removed the third storey and made it into a flat roof. The roof of the library was also removed and made into a large room overlooking the marvellous Burt Castle and surrounding hillside. Tuilagi lived here for many years. I'm unsure on whether he died while in ownership of the rectory or if he had sold the house before he passed on. It continued to change hands through the years before my parents came upon this fabulous house.

Chapter II

Grandparents Alice and Raymond McDaid, mother Lisa and Uncle Raymond moved to Newtowncunningham to settle in 1979. They built their home in Killyverry, five minutes outside the village, where my grandparents still live today. While growing up, Mum heard various stories of a haunted house on Sharon Glebe which is a ten-minute walk from where she lived. The house was well known to the area and local people would tell their stories about the gruesome murders that took place and how they left their imprint within the house. While several families lived in the house throughout the years, some had their own stories of this haunted location. People would see full apparitions, shadows lurking around corners, and experience unexplainable things within certain rooms of the house. The locals had mixed feelings about this mysterious house and with its horrific past it was not surprising that it was forever talked about from generation to generation. The house was left abandoned for years. While it stood alone in a quiet location, groups of people went to the rectory uninvited, and vandalised the structure, stripping it of its character. Local people would gather for ghostly adventures on the dark, cold nights to play the Ouija board or communicate with spirits that haunted the grounds just for the thrill of a scare.

My parents were curious about Sharon Rectory and the amazing stories that they heard throughout their childhood. One bright summer's night in 1988 they decided to venture down the back entrance to Sharon Rectory. The laneway was overgrown with high trees and hedges on each side. As they drove down this narrow laneway, they came to a dead end. There were two white rusted gates that lay between the man-size stone pillars, which blocked the entrance into the grounds. They parked the car tightly against the gate, both slowly building up the courage to get out of the car and explore the ruins of the rectory. Before they came to a decision on whether or not they would get out of the car, they noticed a large black dog running towards the gates. The dog seemed to come from nowhere and was charging directly for the car. Suddenly, it jumped straight through the closed gates and ran up the side of the car, then disappeared. Without hesitation Dad put the car in reverse and backed up the lane towards the main road. When leaving the laneway, they saw a thick rope tied from one side of the lane to the other which hadn't been there previously. While they reversed towards the rope, they noticed it had three large knots tied equally within the length of the rope. While they hadn't noticed the rope crossing the laneway ten minutes before, it seemed strange to say the least. Confused by what had happened, they couldn't explain how this large black dog had been able to run straight through closed gates without hesitation or injuring itself. Later, when they spoke about their experience to people, they were told that a black, red-eyed phantom dog is a hellhound and supposedly had been seen before on the grounds of the rectory. This 'hellhound' seemed very unrealistic, although my parents just laughed about it and thought there had to be some kind of logical explanation. But little did they know this dog would make an appearance again in the future.

Seven years later my parents were looking to purchase a property around the Newtowncunningham or Manorcunningham area. After viewing a few other properties, my grandfather had been talking with a Father O'Reilly who was the current owner of Sharon Rectory. Father O'Reilly agreed for my parents to come and look at the property knowing they would possibly purchase the rectory and turn it into a beautiful home. My parents fell in love with the house once they saw it, but Dad knew it would take a lot of work to restore it. There was a moment where he thought maybe it was best to knock it and build a new home. But Father O'Reilly wouldn't sell the house knowing this would happen. They knew it would take blood, sweat and tears to make the house a home but they were keen on the project. They bought the property in the beginning of 1995 and started the renovations in May of that year. It was an expensive and time-consuming project for my family but once they set eyes on the house, they fell in love with it. I was six years old at the time and was excited to move into this big beautiful house. Mum's father was a builder and agreed to help as much as he could on the renovations. My dad, uncle and grandfather spent weekends and late nights clearing rubble and making the space safe to start building.

I remember the first time I saw Sharon. It looked old, broken and overgrown with grass, weeds and ivy. It was like something straight out of a horror movie. I couldn't imagine it ever being liveable. When I first walked through the halls, the rooms were in ruins, but they each had specific characteristics. I imagined how they once were. It felt like I walked back in time. As a child I had a great imagination, this was a new and exciting adventure, but something didn't feel right with the house. I couldn't wait to check where my bedroom was, so I begged Mum to take me to it. Because the staircase wasn't safe at this stage, we used ladders to go up and down the first level. I couldn't wait to see what upstairs was like.

The first level hallway led on to a large bedroom which was to be my parents' room, and their room led through a smaller bedroom which was my room. The bedrooms had many doors and interconnecting rooms which couldn't be changed due to the way the house was built. But it had its advantages because at least I was a doorway from my parents. There was one door in my bedroom that I couldn't help but feel fear for when I looked at it. It went through to a darkened back staircase which I instantly felt uneasy with. Because the bedroom was next to my parents' and I was still so young, I had to stay in it. The bedroom itself felt okay. There were obvious signs it was once a child's bedroom. The ripped wallpaper had cartoons and it hung off the wall from dampness.

We went downstairs again to one of the larger rooms which the roof had collapsed into. The grass grew up through whatever floor was left. It looked terrifying, because it didn't feel like it was a part of the same house. This room was right next to the kitchen. In here the original tiled floors still laid, untouched and in perfect condition. This was a big piece that my parents wanted to salvage. An old hob cooker stood in the centre of the wall all rusted and dirty, which really put the spook into an old abandoned house!

Raymond and my grandfather worked throughout the week building the structure from room to room. They were at their happiest knowing this project would keep them busy for a while. One occasion, while they worked on the room with no roof, my grandfather spotted what seemed to be bones buried under the grass through the floor. He couldn't tell if they were human or animal. He dug up what looked to be a skull and when he studied it, he knew it was of an animal. When Grandad showed Dad this skull, he thought maybe it was of a sheep. Perhaps it got trapped in there and eventually died. But why would it have been buried so far under the ground? And why was it only the skull that was found? When doing research on their discovery they found that hundreds of years ago in Irish folklore, when building a house there were rules and traditions. Burying a horse's skull in the foundations of the dwelling was believed to bring good luck. When a horse died, they would cut the head off and bury it beneath the threshold. In other traditions period objects such as witches' bottles, shoes and skulls were buried to warn away evil spirits. But at this stage the skull had been removed and without knowing these traditions. This would lead to great consequences for my family through the years.

Raymond had been working outside in the tractor

clearing the overgrown grass from the street. As he worked round the side of the house there were large trees which surrounded the whole area. He accidently hit one of the trees with the tractor but not totally damaging it. He never thought too much of it, to him it was only a tree and it still stood there regardless.

As my dad continued to work every day to pay the bills, my uncle and grandfather continued to work through the week at Sharon. Dad worked in the family business selling tyres and despite all the work he was doing on the house, he would still work the 9 to 5 job. One day, as Dad was fitting a tractor tyre, the wheel blew out on him, knocking him to the ground. As he tried to move, he realised his leg and hip were completely shattered. The other men rushed to his side and phoned for an ambulance. He roared in pain. I was at school when my mum phoned in to take me out early. I was oblivious to what happened to Dad. She left me with my grandmother while she ran to Dad's side. He had been transferred to Sligo Hospital where he had iron rods immediately placed in his hip and leg. He was really lucky to survive. I remember going to hospital to see him days after his accident. This was the last thing my parents needed just after purchasing a house and in the middle of a renovation. It took weeks for Dad to get back on his feet and even that, he was unable to help with the house or work. There was so much pressure on my mum.

Months later, it came up in conversation how Raymond had hit the tree outside and how it was still standing. It was only then that someone mentioned to my parents that the tree that was damaged was actually known to be a fairy tree. When a fairy tree is damaged or cut down, serious consequences are met by the owner of the land or the person who commits such damage. My parents laughed at the craziness of this. Was it a coincidence that days before my dad's accident, Raymond had accidently damaged this tree or was it these 'fairies' that hexed my dad? We will never know.

After a stressful few months prior to Dad's accident, the structural renovations were almost complete and the summer of 1996 quickly crept up before the house was in any way suitable to live in. Dad employed a plumber and electrician so there would be running water, heat and electric to move in before autumn. One evening the plumber was left alone in the house and was working in the downstairs bathroom, fitting the bathroom suite. While he worked, he heard a gush of water coming from behind him. He turned to find the sink which he just fitted had running water coming from each tap. Prior to working on the plumbing that day, he knew he had turned the water off from the outside. So why would the water be coming through the taps? He thought someone had turned on the water outside as a joke knowing he was left alone in the house. He turned off the taps and went outside to check if someone was there. As he looked around the front and the side of the house, he didn't see anyone but noticed the water turned on from the outside. Both the plumber and electrician had experiences while working in the house. They told my parents they would feel unseen eyes watching them or large shadows lurking around corners when nobody else was there. From then, the word of mouth went around about the unexplainable things happening while workers were in the house. This made it difficult to find people to employ to finish the last few jobs before moving in.

The last few weeks had come and gone, and the finishing touches went into each room. Mum started to buy the pieces of furniture to fill the large rooms. They wanted to keep the house authentic, so Mum would often find second-hand shops to buy pieces that were antique or one of a kind. I remembered going to Derry and Letterkenny with her on Saturdays hunting for bargains. She has a great eye for interior and loves bringing her creations to life. In her vision she wanted Sharon Rectory to keep its charter inside and out. The local car boot sales were great; she would buy old oil paintings or small bits and bobs and find the perfect place for them within the house. Everything she bought looked old or had a dated appearance. All that she gathered, would look like it was made for Sharon.

Chapter III

We moved into Sharon on the bank holiday weekend in August of 1996. The first couple of weeks were strange, I suppose it's expected moving into a new house, but something felt different compared to our old home. The atmosphere of the house changed. Each room felt different. It felt like there were eyes watching you when no one else was in the room. I was unaware my parents had been told 'ghost stories' and that the house was haunted, so I was oblivious to why I was feeling like this.

The weeks passed and the evenings grew darker. There was a lot of work that needed to be done within the house. My parents would spend their evenings and weekends painting and decorating the rooms. Even though the house was coming together, I remember feeling cold spots in certain rooms. Not everywhere felt like this but once you entered a particular part of the room, you could instantly feel it. It felt odd, I couldn't explain it and I was too young to understand otherwise. It took us a couple of weeks to feel settled. I was glad my bedroom was directly beside Mum and Dad. Without a doubt I felt scared at night. I couldn't help but sit wide awake looking at the door that led to the back staircase. The door had a small window which was slightly frosted. I would picture in my head someone with a white face looking through the window directly at me as I lay there. My imagination would go into overdrive and I'd scare myself so much that I would struggle to fall asleep.

It wasn't long before school soon started back. Most days I would wake exhausted. I would look forward to finishing so I could get the bus to my grandmother's just so I could lie on her sofa and fall sleep watching telly. Mum would pick me up on her way back from work around six o'clock and we would travel home to the unnerving atmosphere that lay beyond the doors. It wasn't long before my parents realised the house had extra occupants which they didn't expect.

October fell and the night sky would creep in earlier day by day. The laneway felt unsettling as we travelled up and saw the house peering in the distance. It definitely had the Halloween effect. Inside seemed dead quiet, but I still felt scared. I could sense things from room to room. Dad thought it would be a great idea to throw a fancy-dress housewarming. Since Halloween was busy that year as they continued to work on the house, they decided to throw the party at the beginning of November. Everyone my parents knew was invited. People from far and wide came, and all made great efforts with their costumes. A few people approached my parents towards the end of the night who had unexplainable experiences while they were there. Some left wondering if they had really experienced something paranormal or if it was just their imagination. People were scattered throughout the ground level but there was a handful of brave ones that wanted to venture down one by one into the dark, cold cellar.

A few days after the housewarming, I woke one night to sudden footsteps coming up the back staircase. As I peeped my head above the duvet to look at the closed door, I expected one of my parents to walk through. But nothing! They seemed to stop just outside the doorway. I lay there and stared at the small darkened window just above the door. If it was my parents, surely they would have put the light on. Why would they come up those stairs in the dark? I didn't know what time it was, so I jumped out of bed to check if my parents were still in their room, but they were both fast asleep. The fear started to creep over me. I was sure I heard someone coming up those stairs! I started to doubt myself. Maybe I was dreaming, and it felt so real that I convinced myself I heard it? I kept my bedside light on and struggled to fall back asleep. The next day I didn't bother telling Mum. I had clearly dreamt it and was working myself up over nothing. This is what I thought. But from that night, things that I thought I'd imagined, became real.

The next couple of nights I kept my bedside light on. I still felt scared by the previous night's antics. It was a comfort knowing that I had the light in case I woke with another 'nightmare'. As I closed my eyes to fall asleep, I felt a cold breeze blow past my face. I opened my eyes, though I wish I hadn't. I saw a figure of a woman standing towards the end of my bed. She was lucent with a blue glow and I could see the outline of her dress and her long hair which fell each side of her face. But the thing was, I couldn't see a face. There were no eyes, nose, mouth, it just looked blank. I couldn't move for fear. She stood there for what felt like hours. I was scared to blink, shout, move, run! My body just froze. I didn't feel like she wanted to hurt me but to let me know that she was there. Within the moment she was gone. I didn't sleep the rest of that night. I just lay there with my head under the covers, scared to move. I started to sweat, but I couldn't come up for air for the fear of seeing her again. I didn't tell my parents because I didn't want them to think I was making it up. I was hoping it was going to be a one off. But it little did I know, my parents were experiencing this same apparition!

As the nights went on, seeing this lady became a regular thing. I dreaded going to bed at night because I knew she would be standing at the bottom of my bed. Although I never felt threatened by her, I still felt scared. When I told Mum, she didn't seem to give the reaction I expected. She said she believed me but to not worry. This lady meant no harm. Both my parents were experiencing this same thing but didn't tell me. Dad saw her roughly the same time I did. He woke with three knocks on the bedroom window. He jumped up to check, but he couldn't see anything. He was confused. Their bedroom is on the second floor. "How could someone knock on the window?" He opened the window and looked around from above. He couldn't see anything. When he got back into bed, he rolled onto his side to try to fall back asleep. Suddenly, he saw a blue mist glowing right beside him. It hovered between my bedroom door and my parents' bed. He jumped up and put the light on but within an instance it disappeared. He woke Mum in the process. He was convinced someone was in the room. He checked the rest of the house, but there was no one else there, just us. Dad, being a pretty sceptical man, wanted to find the logical explanation before writing it off as paranormal. He didn't believe in the stories of Sharon, to him they were just scary stories. Even though the men working on the renovations would tell him that strange things were happening, he would just laugh and tell them they were crazy. But now, these were two experiences that had happened to him. He began to doubt his beliefs. This made him think. From previously seeing a black dog jump through closed gates years before buying the house, to having an awful accident after Raymond hit a 'fairy tree' on the land, to seeing this blue figure appearing in front of his very eyes. Was there something behind these stories after all?

We were excited to spend the first Christmas in Sharon. Our house is usually the place to go throughout Christmas and the New Year. We had visitors every weekend, family and friends calling for drinks and a catch-up. Honestly, I think my parents were glad to have the company. Unexplainable things were happening on the daily and this 'Blue Lady' began to make her presence known nightly. I think they didn't want to admit they were scared. But the level of activity increased; bulbs started to blow every day for no reason. The only way I can describe it, when you walk into a room, turn on a light – BANG! Suddenly there is a surge of energy too great. The bulb would just blow. You could almost feel the energy within the room building before it happened. Also, from time to time, when I walked into a certain room, I could smell something revolting. The odour would be like something was dead. Whenever I told Mum and she went to check, the smell would go. It wasn't long after I mentioned this, Mum noticed the smell from time to time throughout the house too.

Grandad would come up every night to sit with us until the last person went to bed. He knew about the strange things happening, so I guess he was worried and thought it best to sit with us for the company. One night, as we sat in the kitchen watching telly, we heard a door bang from afar. We looked at each other in shock. Dad plucked up the courage to check. If anything, it sounded like somebody was in the house with us. When he came back, he said, "There were no doors closed? Maybe it was a draft blowing through the house." But I knew they didn't want to say in front of me. When I went to bed, I lay there looking at the creepy window above the door. Envisioning a white face looking back at me. Within the second, I saw blue mist come through the closed door and slowly form in the room. I knew this was her again. I lay down quickly and pulled the duvet over my head. I peeped over the covers to see if she had gone, but she hadn't. I could see the mist form into a lady with a long, old-fashioned dress. She lingered for a couple of seconds before gliding across the room towards the threshold of my parents' room. I wanted to scream, but I couldn't! This seemed to be her pathway on a nightly occurrence.

As the weeks passed her presence grew stronger. I would lie in bed each night hoping I wouldn't see her.

One dreaded night, I felt the bottom of my bed sink like someone had sat beside me. I lay there with the covers over my head. I knew it was her. I didn't look up. I knew she would be sitting there watching me. I heard a very faint sound, like humming. What was she doing? Was she trying to comfort me? *What do I do?* But again, my body froze! It lasted a few seconds as I lay there under the covers. But she soon disappeared. That had been the scariest night for me since we moved in. She clearly was aware of her surroundings. But did she know she was a ghost? Did she think that we were intruders in her home? This was becoming unbearable. All I thought was, *Mum and Dad need to do something.* This house was coming alive. Nightly I would hear the loud footsteps slowly creeping up the back staircase. It sounded like someone with a heavy footing coming up the stairs one by one, BOOM... BOOM... BOOM... until it reached the landing. Once it approached the door, it stopped! I was terrified. I remember lying with the duvet over my head praying to God that I would fall asleep so I wouldn't have to hear or see this thing again.

The mornings were the worst. I would run on little sleep from being up the night before, terrorised by seeing things. Going into school, I wasn't on top form. School became a nightmare! I plucked up the courage one day to tell some of my friends and of course, they laughed. I wanted to burst into tears, but I knew it would make things worse. I quietly went into the toilets during the breaks and cried. When Mum lifted me from Granny's, I told her about the footsteps I heard coming up the back staircase. She sat quietly in the car for a couple of minutes before reassuring me that it was probably nothing. But I knew by her face she didn't know how to react. Things were getting out of control and she knew something needed to be done. There was a big possibility it wasn't only one ghost in the house.

When we came come, we walked into the kitchen to find the chairs pulled out roughly three feet away from the kitchen table. Nobody had been in the house prior, so we were freaked to say the least! Dad didn't long follow. As he came through the door, Mum asked if he had been home at any stage that day but he replied with a quick, "No, and why?" As they looked around nothing else seemed out of place. This happened regularly, but it still didn't make it less terrifying.

Later that evening while we were in the kitchen, a knock came at the back door. A friend of the family who lived close by called for a visit. It was like any other night at Sharon, we always had visitors come and go. When my parents and their guest sat in conversation, without warning the cast-iron rack that stood on the island in the middle of the kitchen started to shake. The wine glasses on the rack began to rattle. The trembling continued. It didn't shake in an aggressive sense but a pulse-like rhythm. Everyone was accounted for and no one was near the island. It sounded like someone was lightly running across the floor in the above room which caused the vibrations. Our guest was stunned! As they talked about what was going on in the house, I overheard Mum tell him about the night she woke and saw the 'Blue Lady'. She stood glowing blue with her flowing dress and her hair pinned up into a bun. She stood beside Dad in the bed. Mum panicked and woke him, but he couldn't see her. Dad put his arm straight out of the side of the bed, waving it back and forth. Mum could see his arm go straight through her. Our guest sat in horror as she continued to tell him the stuff that was happening.

My parents would see her hovering at the bottom of the bed in the early hours of the morning. The trunk at the bottom of the bed would bang like someone kicked it, or the lock attached would rattle. This would be their wake-up call. We all struggled to sleep nightly. Mum begged and pleaded at night for her to leave! But to this spirit, this was HER home. So why should she leave? We would often hear doors slam throughout the night and furniture dragged across the floor. It sounded like the whole room was being rearranged. I started to stay at my grandmother's just so I could get a night's sleep. Mum was so scared at this point. The days she finished work early, she could only make it as far as the kitchen door before turning. She would leave to go to her Mum's until Dad came home from work. My parents didn't know what to do. They had sunk all their money into building this home. It would be a massive loss if they tried for a quick sale. What other options did they have?

Mum took it into her own hands to research the history of Sharon Rectory. She asked the local heritage centres if they had any information on the murders that took place in 1797. They came forward with some documents, but the pieces weren't adding up. She was advised to go to Trinity College in Dublin; they would have the documents she needed on the history and who lived in the rectory as far back as the late 18th century. She continued her own research locally, knowing she wouldn't get the time to make the journey to Dublin anytime soon. Mum knew about the recent history from her parents and talking with many local people that knew of the previous occupants. She discovered who Reverend William Hamilton was and why he was a wanted man by the United Irishmen. But when digging, she uncovered his horrific past. She also found some newsletters and scripts on the Wallers who lived in Sharon in the late 1700s. She continued to research as more and more information unfolded. She found that Mrs Waller had died tragically on the night of the 2nd of March 1797 during the siege for Hamilton. She started to make the connection that this spirit lady we were seeing nightly, possibly was Mrs Waller.

Chapter IV

In the spring of 1997, the house still needed slight work outside. My father asked Raymond and my grandfather if they could do some grounds work in their free time. My parents wanted the house to look presentable when coming up the main driveway. They bedded flowers and planted trees along the laneway and in the front of the house. My grandfather had started to paint the main building, while the rest was all old stonework. It really started to come together. Sharon didn't look as spooky as it once presented itself. Dad suggested on digging a pond at the bottom of the garden. He thought it would be a grand feature for the grounds. He had heard there once was a fishpond on the property many years ago. When asking Raymond for help he was reluctant, but he knew Dad was keen on this feature. Within a few days, Raymond had dug a large hole with the digger. They then lined it and filled with water. It looked beautiful when it was finished. When driving up the laneway, you could see the water glistening as the lane curved before approaching the house. I loved the outdoors. I would follow my dogs and go on adventures throughout the acres surrounding Sharon. I would trail after them as they would run through the pond and swim to the other side. It looked deep, but I knew better not to go near the edge.

Mum wasn't happy with the pond. Although it looked beautiful, she had an awful feeling surrounding it. One night, as she drifted off to sleep, she began to dream.

She was walking out of the front door, looking for me. She called out but I didn't reply. When walking around the side of the house she couldn't see past all the trees. As she ran halfway down the back laneway, she caught a glimpse of me standing at the edge of the pond with the two dogs. She called my name while walking through the trees towards me. Within a second, I was gone. The dogs still stood there at the edge of the water looking in. They barked as the water rippled towards them. Mum ran to the pond screaming my name, "EMMA!" She jumped into the water and searched underneath with both hands trying to feel around for me. Suddenly, she pulled out a pillowcase stuffed with something solid. When she opened it, there I lay curled in the foetal position. I was in this pillowcase as a stillborn baby.

She screamed so loud in her dream she woke herself up. When she shot up in the bed trying to catch her breath, there she saw the Blue Lady at the foot of her bed. She stood with her head slightly tilted and her hands held like she was cradling something. Mum froze! She didn't feel threatened but scared for the nightmare she just experienced. Within a moment she was gone. Disturbed by what had just happened, she couldn't fall back asleep.

The next morning Mum rang her brother Raymond and asked him to fill in the pond. He asked no questions and within a couple of days the pond was gone. Mum believes that Mrs Waller was trying to warn her of this pond. It was going to be a risk to me while I wandered outside, unknowingly seeking the danger that lay ahead. From that moment, Mum was certain that Mrs Waller was no threat to her or our family. She knew she was a protector and only resided there because this was still the home she loved.

Growing up with so much space surrounding my home was a dream. I loved the outdoors. As soon as I came home from school, I was straight outside. One afternoon in May, while I was out walking my dogs, we started to run towards the back laneway. When coming through the darkness of the trees, the dogs started to bark vigorously into the hedge. I stopped and stood there for a moment to see what the dogs were barking at. They seemed agitated and continued to growl and bark at something, or nothing? I was curious and went over to check. I thought it was a cat or a rabbit they had spotted but I couldn't get in close enough to see. When I walked by the hedge, out jumped a large black dog. It was almost twice the size of my dogs. I couldn't believe it! It looked at me with piercing red eyes and it had an aggressive feel about it. I felt it looked into my soul. I shouted at my two dogs to come to me. I was scared that they might challenge this creature to a fight. However, the strange dog turned and ran towards the trees to the back gate. Both my dogs ran after it. They ran through the hedging, barking while looking for it. But it had gone. I couldn't believe what I saw. It had happened so fast that I had to stop and think, *What did I just see?* I doubted myself yet again. But the reactions of my dogs said otherwise. I ran back to the house. I couldn't get in the door quick enough to tell Mum. She stood in shock when I explained what happened. It was only then she told me about her and Dad's experience with this strange dog around 10 years previous before they bought the house. This black 'demon dog' we assumed stalks the grounds. Since experiencing this hellhound, more stories about this creature resurfaced as my parents told friends about what we saw. It seemed that we weren't the only people to have seen this dog on the grounds of Sharon.

Roughly a week later, this demon dog was thing of the past. Yes, it scared me when I saw it, but I didn't let it stop me from spending time outside. One Friday evening after I finished school, I came home, got changed and went straight outside on my bike. As I cycled towards the back lane, I noticed a strange man wearing all black walking towards the house. I stopped as he came towards me. He wore a long black trench coat that seemed to reach his ankles. His black hat slightly shaded his pale face which was expressionless. He almost looked grey in colour. He walked really slowly as he got closer to me. As I stood there watching him, he looked really strange. I had never seen this man before and I didn't know if I should say something or just run and get Mum. As he came closer, I panicked. I shouted over to him, "Are you looking for my dad?" There was nothing. Just silence... After a moment, he turned and slowly began to walk back down the laneway. Within the moment he disappeared. All I could think was, *Why are these strange things always happening to me?* I felt like my days consisted of seeing something, fearing it, then telling my parents. I felt sorry for Mum. I knew she was scared herself and I probably worried her even more. I had to tell her about this strange man in the black coat. Weirdly, I wasn't the only person to see this strange man. When my parents bought the house in the beginning of 1995, during renovations my great aunt kept her horses on the grounds. She often called in on the evenings to check on them in the field beside the back lane. Upon her visit one evening, she walked down the back laneway to the entrance of the field. She couldn't see any sign of her horses, so she jumped the gate and went a few feet into the field. She called them towards the gate, but they seemed to ignore her and grazed on. She waited for a moment before turning to jump over the gate. Just then, she noticed a man wearing a long black coat standing in the middle of the laneway. She thought this was a man looking for my parents and shouted to him, "Can I help you, sir?" But he didn't reply. He stood there for a few seconds before turning and walking away. She told my parents he literally disappeared. She thought it strange but knew Sharon Rectory had history of wandering apparitions and lost souls. I think she saw things as a child while she and my grandfather worked on the grounds of Sharon, but they rarely would talk about what they experienced.

Over the summer holidays, I remember going out shopping with Mum to car boot sales where she would buy beautiful antique pictures and knicks and knacks. She would often find bargains and once she set eyes on them, she would know right away where to put them. The walls stood bare in the large reception room, so it needed paintings for the final touches. She found a beautiful set of illustrations of Greek and Roman mythology. She was dying to get home that evening to see how they looked in the room. I remember watching Dad place them one by one on the wall, measuring the distance between each so they looked perfect. There was one in particular, that stood out to me. I didn't like it. The picture was of several naked women that looked to be sacrificing a person to a lion. I never in the slightest would look in great detail at artwork or what the paintings represented, but this picture disturbed me. To Mum they were paintings that fitted with the character of the rectory. I said to Dad while he was hanging the paintings, "I don't like this picture. It scares me." He laughed and said that we wouldn't be able to listen to Mum if he didn't get all the pictures up. As they lined up on the wall, I couldn't help but constantly stare at this one particular picture. It really bothered me.

That evening while we were having dinner in the kitchen, we heard this almighty bang come from the reception hallway. It sounded like something was thrown to the floor. Dad jumped up to go check and as soon as he reached the reception room, there in the middle of the floor was one of the pictures lying face down. The picture fell about five feet almost to the middle of the room. It looked to have been thrown off the wall because the nail still firmly stood in place. The sound of the fall was expressed like it had force behind it. This was to coincidental. Dad walked over to pick up the picture and as he turned it around, he laughed. It was the picture that I didn't like. We laughed nervously. "The ghosts must have heard me saying I didn't like that picture." Both Mum and Dad looked at each other in misbelief. When placing the picture back up on the wall we went back to finish our dinner. The next morning, when Dad came down the front staircase, he walked into the reception hallway to find the same picture had been laying on the floor face down in the same place. After this, he put the picture in storage. This was a sign they needed to respect the spirits and my feelings on this painting. At least they were on my side.

Since moving into the house, nearly all the electrical equipment throughout would turn itself on and off. My computer that sat in the corner of the bedroom, would switch on without me anywhere near it. It would happen day or night. The desktop screen would load, then within a second it would cut off. Whatever spirits were in the house were obviously manipulating these devices to build up their energy to manifest or move something. Of course, I didn't know any of this then. I was just terrified of it happening. Most evenings the lights would dim to the point where they nearly switched off. It would be so dark in the room you could directly look at the bulb without hurting your eyes. More and more unexplainable things were happening, and it was becoming so draining. While I often had friends come to keep me company, they too were sometimes scared of what would happen from time to time. I think when I told them the stories, this played havoc with them during their visits. They would come over to play but often were too scared to have a sleepover. I would jump at the chance of going to their houses just so I could get away from all the unpleasantness of what I experienced.

I remember it was late one summer's night, I lay in bed and heard one of the doors slam forcefully shut from somewhere in the house. It echoed throughout the place. This wasn't the first time we heard the doors bang at night, but I felt more on edge with this. It had a sinister, forceful sound behind it. While other times it would sound like someone was closing a door behind them, this was as if someone charged out of the room slamming a door as they walked out. It seemed to come from the hallway by the sitting room or patio area. I could hear one of my parents get up and walk towards the hallway to the front staircase. I assumed one of them was going to check what banged. Shortly after, I heard the footsteps coming back into their bedroom as though they were getting back into bed. I was scared to close my eyes and fall asleep for the rest of the night. It got to the point where I feared it might harm one of us. I knew this wasn't the Blue Lady but something with a much greater force. This was a warning or intentionally done to cause disruption.

When in the kitchen, Dad often sat in the old armchair that stood in the corner of the room just beside the door to the downstairs bedroom. We would often feel a gush of cold air move from this doorway straight through the room to the opposite door out the hall. It wasn't a draft, but more a swirling breeze. It felt like a mini tornado would pass through the room. One evening as Dad sat in his armchair, myself and Mum sat on the sofa just across from him. As we watched TV, Mum's eye caught a glimpse of a blue mist that seemed to appear behind Dad. Mum said to him, "I think she is standing behind you." He could feel the coldness around him but didn't feel threatened. I could see a blue aura surrounding him. It was as clear as day. Since my parents had their suspicions that this was Mrs Waller, they knew she meant no harm. It would still alarm us when we saw her. However, I didn't feel as scared of her when my parents were there. Why she stood there behind Dad, we don't know. Maybe she took a shine to him? He was now the man of the house. Perhaps she felt it was her duty to care for him like she did her husband?

Chapter V

It's mid-August 1997. It's been a year since we moved into the house, and a tough year it was. We still lay awake at night waiting for things to happen, unsure of what is going to happen next. Mum had exhausted all solutions for what they could do regarding these paranormal experiences. We knew there was good in the house but going by some of the more frightening experiences we couldn't guarantee all was good. My Grandma Tully told my parents to get the house blessed by a priest. It was worth a try and it couldn't possibly make things any worse. That weekend Mum went to see the local priest to find out if he would conduct a house blessing. He agreed and times were arranged. We patiently waited for his call. When the priest came to Sharon, he walked through the house, room by room, conducting a blessing in each one. I could see his reaction; he could sense something there, but he didn't say anything. He continued to do the blessing. When he left, everything seemed still. Too still for my liking. Things settled for a few days. But it wasn't long before everything started to happen again. This time, something seemed angry. Knowing the haunting was becoming worse, my parents needed to seek advice from someone with knowledge of hauntings.

As word got out about our paranormal experiences, people thought my parents were mad. Sharon Rectory was the talking point from near and far. So much so, even the local radio station reached out. They hoped my parents would go on air to tell them our story. It was only going to go two ways. Either people would believe and offer advice and knowledge on hauntings, or people would think we were making it all up. My parents went live on air, to talk about how the haunting progressed as time went on. They explained how we each saw this apparition of a 'Blue Lady' and the ghostly footsteps that could be heard throughout the house. But the astonishing part was, how furniture and other objects would be moved within the house. If we wanted to continue to live in the house peacefully, we needed to put to rest whatever unsettled souls walked among us. Seeing this as an opportunity, Dad asked if any listeners knew anyone who might be willing to help. I vaguely remembered the people's reactions within the radio station. No doubt they thought it was a load of bull.

Surprisingly, shortly after our interview many people had come forward to the radio station, telling them their ghostly experiences and how they related to our story. It was surprising how many people believed us and knew of people that could help.

After the radio interview, a few people had got in touch with my parents that were willing to help or give advice. Someone had suggested getting in touch with a man from Dublin who would travel up and sus out the root of the problem. In the meantime, after hearing my parents on the radio, Anita, one of Mum's friends got in contact, explaining that a mutual friend knew of a lady from Strabane that could possibly help. With Strabane being much closer than Dublin Mum gave the go-ahead to forward on her phone number. She had hope this could possibly be the person that would finally be able to give us answers. A couple of days later, they got in touch with a lovely lady called Kate Houston. Kate was a psychic medium and had previous experience dealing with hauntings. Her first visit to Sharon would definitely be one that she wouldn't forget.

When Kate got in touch, she agreed to visit almost straight away. Anxious, Mum didn't know what to expect. No-one knew what to expect of this! Kate arranged to come to the house with Anita and another lady. When the night had come for Kate's first visit, I asked to stay at my grandmother's because I didn't want to know what Kate picked up. I didn't want to feel more scared than I already was. As Anita, Kate and their friend drove up the front laneway, Kate instantly began to pick up something unsettling. They got halfway up the lane to the house when the car suddenly stopped dead. Yes, DEAD!! There was no particular reason for this malfunction. The engine refused to start, and the lights wouldn't turn on. They sat there in complete darkness. They started to freak out. After a few moments, they gathered themselves and continued to turn the ignition. But still there was nothing. It was puzzling to them why this was happening. Kate had a daunting feeling that whatever awaited her, prevented her from entering the house. Finally, after numerous tries the car started again. This was very strange to them. It didn't make sense. There was no previous car trouble, so why did this suddenly happen? And why on route to Sharon Rectory?

My parents waited in the kitchen expecting them any moment. Suddenly, they heard a loud shout for "HELP...!" It seemed to come from the upper hallway. Mum and Dad looked at each other confused. Within a moment the kitchen door opened. There, Kate and the two ladies walked in. They sighed with relief.

Mum asked, "Why did you shout for help when coming in the door? Are you okay?"

The three of them nodded with disagreement.

Anita said, "No, we for shouted LISA!" This was only the beginning of a very eventful night.

When everyone introduced themselves, Kate offered reassurance that she would try her best to get to the root of the haunting. She didn't want to know about the history. All she wanted to know was where the most active parts of the house would be. Mum explained, it was through the whole building. But mainly within the back staircase, the bedrooms and the kitchen. These were the rooms we mainly used. They told her our experiences, the banging of doors, phantom footsteps, bulbs blowing, the awful odour that would follow from room to room, the moving of furniture – day and night. This was only the half of what we were experiencing. As Mum listed them out, she began to realise how much we actually experienced throughout the year. It felt like a never-ending horror movie. Mum clarified how both Dad and I saw this Blue Lady around the same time. She began to appear nightly at the foot of each bed.

Firstly, Kate felt drawn to the room beside the front door. This was once known as the sunroom parlour. When she walked up the hallway, she could sense a lot of individuals rushing, like residual energy. She passed the hall that led to the cellar and patio doorway. "I will come back to this area," said Kate. She walked into the room. This was my dad's 'mancave'. He had a pool table, slot machines, bar, jukebox, you name it. But when they entered the room, it was ice cold. They could see their breath as they spoke. This wasn't a coldness in the usual sense, this was more a sudden drop in temperature.

Anita sat on the large windowsill and the rest stood separately throughout the room. Suddenly, Anita felt two arms pull her towards the glass in the window. She jumps up with a scream. "WHAT THE HELL WAS THAT?" They stood in shock. This was validation to everyone there that something paranormal was definitely at work here. Kate could sense death linked with the house. Great loss and suffering. She could see a woman fall to her knees gripping in pain. She started to envision the scenes from that fateful night. She could see Mrs Waller stooping from gunfire. The gunshots came through the windows in this particular room. Kate continued to describe in detail.

Mum caught a glimpse of the 'Blue Lady' out the corner of her eye. She stood within the hallway watching as her story unfolded. Before Mum could speak, Kate promptly said, "She is here, watching us." This confirmed that the 'Blue Lady' was Sara Waller, the previous Lady of Sharon Rectory. It all started to make sense to my parents. The history they knew was beginning to intertwine as she confirmed from room to room.

Kate continued to tell them, "There is more than

one spirit here." She moved to the hallway and stood beside the cellar door. "I can pick up a male spirit, he is a very angry man. There is a lot of politics surrounding his death." Kate started to feel drained. My parents thought it best for her to have a break and come back another time to finish the tour. It was an interesting night and the information Kate was picking up was weirdly accurate. This really surprised my parents. They were very sceptical to psychic mediums before meeting Kate. But she really changed their views. The things Kate spoke about were difficult for my parents to find out, never mind a person who didn't know the area or the name of the house. She really seemed legit. There was hope for us yet. Could this lady really be the person that could actually help?

Raymond was intrigued by our experiences. When Mum told him the things that were happening, he wanted to see and experience this for himself. In that same week, he had asked if he could stay for a night. He felt a connection to the house, like something drew him there. Raymond is a very quiet man but has a bubbly personality. To me he always seems fearless. He is the type of person to stand in the middle of a thunderstorm and watch the lightning as it struck. Both him and Mum get on very well. They are similar, both quiet and lovely people. Mum offered for Raymond to stay in the downstairs bedroom. But I think she thought it would be funny to see Raymond's reaction if he experienced something. Curious, she wanted to see how he felt when the lights went out. As night fell, Raymond was like a Cheshire cat. The room he was supposed to sleep in was off the kitchen downstairs. Mum and I went upstairs to go to bed. Just when I started to drift off to asleep, I woke with footsteps coming from the back staircase. I clenched my duvet pulling it over my head, hoping it wasn't the notorious spirit that made its presence known frequently. My bedroom door opened ever so gently. I was that scared I couldn't look. Then I heard a voice. It was Raymond. I felt somewhat relived. He asked to go through to Mum's room. I knew he looked scared. I wondered to myself if he had seen something downstairs that spooked him. He walked through the room and knocked on my parents' door. Mum shouted to come in. I got up and went into the room behind him. He asked if he could stay on their bedroom floor. He wanted to see this apparition that we saw nightly. We thought he was crazy. He wanted to see this ghost and we were the complete opposite. Mum got blankets from the hot press and made a makeshift bed on the floor. I thought, *Well I'm definitely not sleeping on my own tonight neither.* I slept between Mum and Dad.

There, the four of us lay awake in the almost darkened room dreading in case she appeared. I think

Mum was glad of Raymond's company. Even though Dad didn't show fear as such, you could feel the uneasiness within the room. We waited as we were expecting for something to happen. I lay awake for what seemed like hours. But I must have fell asleep shortly after. Raymond tossed and turned as he lay awake on the floor. He stared up at the ceiling and looked around the room patiently waiting to see this ghost lady. Unexpectedly, he saw a pink light appear in the corner of the room. He sat up to study it and looked around to see where the light was coming from. The dim glow from the light of the dresser-wardrobe shone ever so slightly. My parents kept this on at night, just so we weren't in complete darkness. This strange pink anomaly floated above the door in the corner of the room. *It couldn't have been from the light,* he thought. He sat up to check if we were awake, but we were fast asleep. Within seconds the pink light started to get bigger and brighter. He couldn't understand where the light was shining from and why it glowed pink. He couldn't keep his eyes off it. The light shone bright towards him like a stream from across the room. Then it shot straight towards him. He lay there frozen for what seemed like hours. Whatever force had a hold of him left within a couple of minutes. Needless to say, Raymond lay awake for the rest of the night. For my parents and I, it was the first night in weeks that we slept through until morning.

Chapter VI

Kate's second visit was arranged a few days after Raymond's stay. This was so she could walk the full house and grounds. As she came through the door, Kate could instantly sense the presence of Mrs Waller. She felt as if her spirit guided her from room to room. Before the beginning, Kate made it clear again that she didn't want to know anything about the history. She didn't want to feel influenced on the energies as she walked through the house. The only thing she did know was that the Blue Lady was Sara Waller. Mum and I wanted to walk along with Kate just to see what she was going to pick up. She began to walk from the front porch into the reception room. You could see in her face; she began to feel other presences among us. She felt like she was being pulled from room to room. It was almost overwhelming. She walked into the sunroom parlour, which we called the bar. But Kate was picking up the name of the room that once was. When we walked into the room and stood quietly, we could hear the rustling of clothing. Mrs Waller's presence felt strong in this room. Kate closed her eyes as she envisioned men outside this room's window. They seemed angry. She could hear shouting and chanting, like they wanted something within the house. Within a second Mum burst into tears. It was an overwhelming feeling that came over her. She didn't feel sad or upset before, but a charge of energy surged through her and seemed to circle the room like a hurricane swirling around. Kate ever so gently held Mum's hands and asked her to breathe and not fight the reaction. Mum began to calm. She didn't know what happened. She had never experienced anything like this before! As she sat down, Kate kneeled in front of her and explained that it was the fear and sadness that Mrs Waller suffered the night she died. What happened that night, couldn't be undone. It brought great sorrow for the household. I was shaking. It was all surreal. They asked if I wanted to go to Granny's, but I said, "No." I wanted to stay and see what would happen next.

We walked towards the large sitting room. I love this room. It's one of my favourite rooms to spend time in over Christmas. It always felt homely with the blazing fire, the Christmas decorations and the tree lit up in the corner. But when we walked into the room, it felt like we entered another house. Everything even looked different. It's so hard to explain how it feels to walk into a room you know and not recognise it. The atmosphere was heavier. The room looked a dark grey and felt so cold. The whole house was freezing. Kate walked in the room and straight out of the other door at the opposite end. This led to the patio hallway. As soon as she put her foot over the threshold it was like she hit a brick wall. We looked in confusion. Mum knew from her research this was where one of the murders took place. But this wasn't to Kate's knowledge. She stood beside the door, closed her eyes and took a deep breath in. "Something happened here. Something really bad." We stood in the hallway and suddenly, it felt like a swift breeze passed us. It was like something had rushed from the cellar door to the patio doorway. Kate pointed to the door and said, "I need to leave this room to last." The energy seemed so strong in hallway. It felt heavy. It was almost impossible to breathe.

We walked upstairs. As Kate got to the top she turned to the wall and said, "I feel like I need to keep going up."

Mum replied, "There used to be another floor level, but it was demolished and made into a flat roof by one of the previous owners."

We continued to walk down the hall leading to my parents' bedroom. Kate laughed as we walked into the room. She looked at Mum. "I love that you're hiding the suitcases under the bed." It was weird because the bed clothes draped over the sides so you couldn't see anything that hid under the bed. She sensed grief in this room. Mum knew that a lady and her baby had both passed away in the master bedroom. My grandfather told her about this tragic incident with the previous occupants when they bought the house. You could feel the sadness within the room. Kate added, "The spirits in the house are all from different timelines." Some of the activity that was happening was residual. The spirits are in a constant loop. Replaying their last days over and over. Usually a residual haunting often happens where a tragic death occurred. It's almost like an imprint was left after they passed.

My room was next. I was dreading it because all I could think was, *What bad thing happened in my room?* Every room so far had a tragic story associated with it. Kate walked through the door. She smiled and looked at me. "Your room has such a lovely feel to it." Right then, it felt like the warmest room since we began our walkthrough. I was so glad she didn't pick up anything negative. I told her about the spooky window above the door and how I imagined a pale white face lurking at me while I tried to sleep. She opened the door and looked down the stairs.

Kate asked if I ever heard footsteps coming up the

stairs. "Yes, nearly every night," I said. "Sometimes they sound so heavy. They really scare me."

She walked into the bedroom opposite my room. Mum walked over to fix the bed. "This bed would annoy me. I come in every day to fix it. I don't know why. But it's like something keeps laying on it." I often got the blame for it. Even though I would never be in that room. Something scared me in there. It seemed that as I got closer to this end of the house, it got scarier.

Kate could see someone lying on the bed. She pointed. "That's your culprit there."

We looked around. "Where?" we said.

"There is a man that comes in and lies on this bed," Kate replied. Freaked out by this, we carried on downstairs. Under the staircase is a small room. In here is a small rusted sink called a jaw box. The servants would have used it for washing their face and hands. I never liked the feeling in there. It is extremely claustrophobic, it's a small, narrow room that a child would barely get moving in. This was the servants' quarters. Kate looked at me. "Emma, the reason you keep hearing footsteps coming up the stairs is because the servants would have used them daily. It's a residual energy. The heavy footsteps are probably of the spirit that lies on the bed upstairs. He seems to have a strong presence." I couldn't believe at this point the amount of ghosts we had in the house.

Kate felt Mrs Waller there through the whole walk through. Every room we entered we could feel the constant coldness whirl among us. When Kate reached the kitchen, she felt a busy atmosphere. There was a lot of energy flowing back and forth. She could feel the same type of energy from her first visit. Again, this was residual. It wasn't a bad or negative feeling. This room is the soul of the house. Mrs Waller still sustained a strong presence throughout the whole house. She seemed to be a protector.

We walked back up the hallway towards the reception room. Kate continued to the cellar. She slowly opened the door to venture down. I hated the cellar and still do. Every time I walk past the door my heart starts to race and I get shivers through my whole body. It's a dark, cold and horrific place. I know most cellars and basements tend to have a general eerie feel, but this one is different. There is something really evil and hostile that's in there. Kate felt a pull towards the door like whatever was down there wanted her. Both Mum and Kate went down, while I stood at the door. Kate asked for me to stay put. Whatever malevolent entity lingering within its walls has the energy to jam the door shut. Obviously, I stayed put, I was too frightened to go down. I'm not sure what happened while down there, but I could hear strange sounds from above. Like gurgles or growls and I could hear a scratching coming from somewhere within the hallway. I never heard these sounds before. Roughly ten to fifteen minutes later, they came back up. Mum seemed startled. I think after the walk with Kate, it really made her question what was going on. We seemed to have so many lost souls that were stuck. Mrs Waller was tired. She needed help. Her reaching out to us nightly, was her way of communicating to us. It became so surreal for my parents. They were never really believers in the paranormal or psychics, but Mum was taken aback by everything Kate had picked up. She knew Kate wouldn't have known about Sharon's tragic past. It was it difficult for her to find anything on the house. It's not like today where you can use the internet to research. This was too much of a coincidence for her to know in detail what was happening.

Kate wanted to walk outside. We went to the back door and entered into the courtyard. The outbuildings still lay in ruins. Dad used them for sheds to store tools and machinery. She walked in and out of each one. She took deep breaths as she walked. When she reached the end of the courtyard, she couldn't breathe. "Someone died from hanging." She couldn't pinpoint where it was that it happened, but it was in one of the outhouses. This wasn't knowledge to Mum, but it was something she wanted to find out.

We walked beside another doorway into a shed. "Was this room used for horses a one time?" Kate questioned. Mum didn't really know, but again she wanted to find out.

In another outhouse she could sense young children. They ran in and out of the doorway. "A family lived here." Kate smiled as she walked towards the threshold. When she entered the room, things changed. "There was a dark past link with this part of the building. This room holds a dark nature of abuse and abandonment, secrets of mistreatment, violence and hostility towards children." Again, it felt really heavy like it had during some parts of this walkthrough. It physically made me feel sick. I never felt this way when I was in here before. It was like all the energies throughout the house came alive with Kate being there. The whole place felt different. I saw it in a different light. This frightening and mysterious house that I called home, was beginning to unravel. It told its story through Kate as we walked.

She continued though each outbuilding. She felt different energies as she entered each. The shed at the opposite corner of the courtyard, had a pit underground where the previous owners must have worked on machinery. This was Dad's shed. His tools were lined up on shelves along the wall. A wooden ladder which led up to the second floor lay against the wall in the corner. Upstairs had overgrown ivy crawling up the walls through to the roof. The floor wasn't safe, so we couldn't walk on it. Kate claimed up the ladder so she could peer down into the room without going all the way up. What she picked up was nothing from the past but from the future. Which was strange. She warned us not to let anyone walk on the second floor. She could see someone fall through the floorboards. This didn't mean anything to us at the time, but later it would make sense.

We walked through the arch towards the front of the house. Kate felt there were hidden treasures on these grounds. "It would be great if you got a metal detector and walked throughout the grounds to see what you'd find." While walking towards the front of the house Kate stopped as though she saw someone. She stood quietly for a moment. I looked at Mum. "There is a man here who can't pass over. He is overwhelmed with guilt. He didn't die here but is struggling to move on."

Mum asked, "Who was this? Why was he here if he did not die here?"

Kate answered, "He is one of the United Irishmen. He was here the night of Mrs Waller's death. He was the one who fired the shots that killed her. He continues to blame himself for her murder. He's pleading for forgiveness, so he can move on."

Mrs Waller could never see this man even though they were both dead. They seemed to pass each other. Even though he died years later and miles part, he held this regret throughout his lifetime and now through death. He was not able to rest in peace until he had Mrs Waller's mercy. Kate sat as she tried to communicate with both spirits. She needed to channel one, so they communicate. I felt sorry for this spirit. He obviously was stuck for many years after death, haunted by his penance. It was over within a few minutes. Kate helped this man pass. He was no longer grounded to this realm.

We made our way back to the kitchen. Mum asked, "What do we need to do next to help clear the house?" This haunting wasn't as straight forward. Kate would try her best but there was a chance that it wouldn't work. There were many spirits within the house, and some would refuse to leave. My parents were willing to try anything at this point. It seemed like there was no other option. We weren't going to be pushed out of our forever home. Kate suggested a séance. She thought it was the best way to communicate with the spirits, to try help them find peace. We called it a day and Kate said she would be in touch. It really took it out of her. She was physically, mentally and spiritually drained. This was only the beginning of a very long and bumpy road.

Chapter VII

A news reporter who had been in touch with my dad in the recent weeks asked if she could write an article on our ghostly experiences. She heard my parents' radio interview and wanted to find out more on what was happening. Mum and Dad weren't comfortable with the thought of our business circulating around in the newspapers. This was a sensitive subject and he didn't want articles written making a mockery of our experiences. This was very real and a difficult time for my family. When he declined the journalist's request, she respected that this was a difficult situation, but wasn't willing to let this opportunity go. At least when they talked on the local radio station, they had full control of what was being discussed. With a written article Dad was worried in case they twisted his words. People who already knew and spoke about the haunting scoffed and joked about us behind our backs. This frustrated my parents. Nobody realised the strain and stress this caused for myself and my parents. Both grandparents worried for us and what would happen next. I was being bullied by older kids in school. They laughed and taunted me as they heard the stories from other people. Even though my friends knew it was true, some still doubted me.

About two weeks later, the journalist got back in touch. She tracked down my dad at work and when confronting him she told him our story was remarkable. If he agreed to let her write this article it could help others that were going through the same thing. She seemed genuinely curious on our story and wanted to tell it just how we described. My parents finally agreed to let her write the story, but there was one condition, she was to join in the séance.

On the Wednesday night before the séance, my computer seemed like it had a mind of its own. It turned itself on and lit up bright in the corner of the room. I woke up with the glow shining towards my bed. The screen was blank, it didn't show the usual text when starting up, but a plain white screen. It was strange to me because the screen never seemed that bright before. Maybe because the room was darker. The light on my bedside table seemed dimmer than usual. It was like something had turned the bulb down to the lowest setting, but my light wasn't of that sort. I sat up in the bed and thought, *Why is the screen doing that?* The computer had turned itself on many times before, I knew 'something' powered it on there and then. It usually turned itself off again. As I sat there staring at the screen, I could make out a dark shape form within it. It looked like a blurry face. I could make out the eyes, nose and mouth. I was too scared to get up and turn it off. I lay down and pulled the covers over my head. I hid under the blankets until I fell asleep. On the same night Dad woke, with a pressure weighing him down in the bed. He felt a strong force holding him into the mattress. He couldn't move or speak to wake Mum. He began to feel himself slide down in the bed like something was pushing him to the bottom. He started to pray hoping this thing would loosen its hold. Once this force backed off, he jumped up and glanced around the room in terror. Mum lay there asleep, oblivious to what just happened. He knew there was a greater more negative force at work here, not the 'Blue Lady'. From that moment Dad felt threatened in the house.

On Thursday the 11th of September 1997, it felt like any other day. But today, things would change for each person that was involved with the séance. We prepared for Kate to come and conduct the vigil. She and my parents agreed they would hold the séance in the dining room. There was plenty of space and the table was big enough to fit everyone comfortably around it. The idea of the séance was to try to help

Kate and my parents communicate with the spirits and encourage them to cross over. The energy within the house was like a whirlpool spinning from room to room. It almost made you feel lightheaded and sick.

There was a lot of preparation involved. My grandmother Alice and Uncle Raymond were invited to assist on the night. Kate needed family and loved ones to help. Their positive energies would help protect against any negative spirits or entities that were lurking within the shadows. From what Dad experienced the night before, he was apprehensive of what lay ahead. They could sense an adverse impression within the house. Kate ensured the positive and good energies together would form a protection from any evil that would attempt to enter during the séance. Kate would guide and tutor everyone through this. We were nervous; no one knew what a séance entailed. Never in a million years would we have guessed what would happen as we prepared that day. Kate came with a friend who was a white witch and had experience dealing with haunted locations. She felt the need for backup. This was going to be a long and draining night. The journalist, of course, couldn't wait to experience this unique situation. Everyone gathered in the kitchen as Kate explained how the séance worked.

As the night sky grew dark, the house became quiet. The full moon shone brightly through the large windows of the library, sitting room and dining room. It was for the best that the séance was held at night; most activity happened once the lights went out and of course there were less distractions. It's believed that the gravitational pull of the full moon heightens spiritual activity and increases physic powers. I never understood this at the time. As I get older and understand more about the paranormal, it made perfect sense. When I look back, the activity was at its worst when the moon was full. Even to this date the activity rises. Kate and her friend walked around the house prompting the spirits to come out and talk with them. The journalist walked behind taking pictures as they went from room to room. Some of the rooms felt cold with a damp, musty smell. These were the rooms that had the most activity. Kate encouraged the spirits to come forward and follow on to the dining room. Unknowingly to them, this was the room that my grandfather found the skull buried within the ground. Could this be the reason these spirits were drawn to the house? The skull seemingly protected the house against bad luck and warned away evil according to Irish folklore. Was it because there was no form of protection anymore? Would this explain why there were so many other spirits attached to the grounds? We knew the 'Blue Lady' was the spirit of Mrs Waller and that her life was tragically ended within the house. Her soul still seemed grounded to the earth's plane.

When it was time for the séance, everyone that was involved sat comfortably in a circle around the large oval table. Dad and I sat in the kitchen. The house was in complete darkness. It was so terrifying, everything seemed different once the lights went off. Dad sat quietly in his armchair front of the old brown stove. Tall white candles stood from corner to corner around the kitchen. Candlelight was the only light allowed during the night. The dining room was also in darkness, apart from the one candle that was placed in the middle of the table. I remember lying down on the sofa with a fluffy blanket wrapped around me. There was no television, no radio, no lights, nothing! Everything was still and dead silent. The flicker of the candlelight glowed around the kitchen. It seemed like the silence would be disrupted at some point. We waited patiently for something to happen. We began to hear Kate talking from the dining room. Dad suddenly got down on both his knees and prayed.

After a few minutes, the door behind the big armchair in the corner slowly opened wide and closed again. We could feel something in the room with us. It was ice cold. The coldness seemed to move slowly through the room. It was just like the tornado of energy that we frequently felt in the kitchen. The door at the opposite end going out to the hallway was tightly shut. Dad had closed it just before they began the session. Unexpectedly, it began to open. We thought it may have been someone from the séance, but no. No-one was there. The door opened so slowly until it was fully ajar. After a few seconds it started to close, then BANG. It closed shut. I was absolutely terrified. Dad just continued to pray with his eyes closed the whole time. Kate told him before the séance, "Regardless of what activity happens, you need to continue praying."

Kate, Mum, Granny, Raymond and the white witch sat in a circle holding hands around the table. The journalist stood back and watched as the activity unfolded. Kate began a protection prayer to surround the house, grounds and everyone within it. This would protect them from any harm and navigate entities while they communicated with the spirits of the house. They closed their eyes and called forth the spirits within the house. They waited for a few moments in silence. It was as if time stood still. You could hear a pin drop. Kate continued to encourage the spirits to come forward. As they waited, Kate began to pick up on Mrs Waller. She saw the figure of a woman walk through the dining room door. "I see her, she is beautiful." Kate began to describe her. "She has her hair in a bun with ringlets either side, her features are fine. She has blue eyes, with a pale white face. She's wearing a long baroque dress, blue with ruffles and a white collar." At this point no one else could see her, only Kate. Mum couldn't believe how she described her. This was the same woman we saw. Though none of us could never see her face.

Kate continued, "Mrs Waller, is that you? Come join us." The room grew ice cold. "Raymond, she is walking towards you, so please be vigilant." Raymond could feel a connection to Mrs Waller.

Suddenly, my granny heard a gunshot. It sounded as if it was just outside the room. She quickly responded, "What's that noise? It sounds like a gunshot!" She didn't have the words out of her mouth when Kate clutched her shoulder, feeling a sharp burning pain. As soon as Mum turned to her aid, she abruptly burst into tears; it was uncontrollable. She couldn't stop! This continued.

Kate, still flinching in pain, shouted, "Don't break the circle!"

Raymond sat quietly despite everything going on. They composed themselves after a few minutes. The journalist couldn't believe what was happening before her very eyes. Kate looked up. She could see Mrs Waller standing behind Raymond. He never moved. It looked like he was in a total trance. His forehead began to drip with sweat and the blood drained from his face. Kate continued to talk. "Mrs Waller we want to help you. We want to reunite you with your beloved husband and your loved ones. Please can you step into the circle and we can guide you to your forever peace."

The room stood still. Everyone looked at Raymond. Kate could see Mrs Waller move away from him. As soon as Mrs Waller left him, Raymond's head hit the table. He blacked out. Everyone was worried, and Mum shouted for Dad. I remember, I had fallen asleep on the sofa but woke with all this commotion. Dad ran out of the hallway to the dining room. He saw Raymond laying with his head on the table. He shook him, but there was no response. His forehead was boiling. Mum and Granny started to panic. Dad lifted him and dragged him into the bathroom. He sat him at the edge of the bath and dabbed the cold water over his head. Raymond slowly started to come around. He was confused by what went on. He didn't remember anything. "I could see myself standing at opposite end of the room," Raymond said shakily. His body was in shock.

Regardless of all that went on, Kate needed to finish the séance and she needed everyone who started with her to close it. Reluctant, Raymond knew he had to finish it. They sat back around the table and asked for Mrs Waller to come forth again. It took a while, but they could feel the temperature drop in the room. They could see a blue lucid mist float above in the middle of the table. The mist began to form into the shape of a teardrop. They all looked with astonishment. Everyone there could see her. Within a moment she had gone. Kate closed the séance and thanked everyone for their hard work.

Mum walked into the kitchen and turned on the lights. It was just after 3am. Everyone was exhausted. Since they had started earlier that day, it was to be expected that everyone would leave physically, spiritually and mentally drained. We thanked Kate. It was the most surreal experience each person had witnessed. Kate explained Mrs Waller relived her last memories within the circle. That's why we all experienced different things. My granny heard the gunshot, Kate felt her physical pain, Mum felt her overwhelming sadness and Raymond, well, Mrs Waller tried to channel through him. Seemingly she had a connection to Raymond. Was this the reason he always felt drawn to Sharon? It was amazing listening to each person's experience. I could hear all the commotion but didn't understand what was going on. It was a scary but somewhat unbelievable night. But would this finally be the end of the all that happened within the house? It wasn't long before we'd find out.

A couple of days after, my grandmother was out for a stroll along the road in Killyverry. She bumped into her neighbour who asked her, "What was going on up at Sharon Rectory a few nights ago?"

My granny seemed confused. "Why?" she asked.

He replied, "I struggled to get to sleep on Thursday night, so I got up and took a walk outside the house. I could see a strange beam of light shot up into the sky. It looked to be coming from the roof of Sharon."

My granny was shocked. She knew what he had seen, but to confirm she asked, "What time did you see this at?"

He responded, "Oh, must have been around three in the morning, Alice."

When people found out about the séance in Sharon, a lot were very critical and spoke harshly about our experiences. They suggested it was satanical and that we dabbled in something dark. Some people made rumours about my parents taking drugs and hallucinating. Nobody understood what we were going through. It was so hurtful hearing what was said about my family. Whenever I went back to school, I got weird looks from the other students. I could hear their whispers among each other. It was intimidating. Older students would ask me, "Is your house haunted? What did you see? Were you not scared? Why don't you move out?" I didn't know what to tell them because I honestly wanted to move on and forget about the last year. Within a week everyone seemed to be talking about my family and the house. Our close friends were great. They would put people straight who would make remarks or laugh about our experiences. There were some who were very interested in our story and genuinely wanted to know what happened.

A couple of weeks had passed. Sharon Rectory seemed quiet yet again. A lot of the activity had stopped. It was finally over. Well, that's what we thought!

Chapter VIII

As time went on, the night of the séance soon became a distant memory. We wanted to carry on as normal. Mum and Dad showed a slight sense of relief. Mum managed to stay at home on her own without feeling the same fear she once had. There was always a considerable doubt that something else lurked among us. But it wouldn't make itself known as of yet. There was an eerie feeling that lingered in the house. You could still feel the unseen eyes watching while we walked into a room. It felt like something crossed into your aura which gave shivers throughout your body. Something else was here and we didn't know what it was. It felt different than before. I knew it wasn't over. I began to see dark shadows dart past me out of the corner of my eye. It would happen while I was in the kitchen or when I lay in bed at night. I said to Mum, "It's happening again." But she didn't seem surprised. Seeing these apparitions became a regular thing over the coming weeks. We all started to see them. You could feel a presence among us, but it didn't feel like Mrs Waller. It felt malevolent. It was being sneaky, watching us, waiting to pounce when we least expected.

The summer of 1998 soon approached, and the nights were beautifully bright. I had just started my school holidays and loved having my friends over for company. We often played outside and ran through the fields at the back of the house. We wandered around pretending to go on adventures through the overgrown grass and trees. Often, we would find treasures buried under grass and muck at the side of the house. A dirt path beside the small stable leading into a field was where we found old clay pots, glass bottles and pieces of broken china. I gathered what I could and took them in to Mum. She wondered why all these were buried at the side of the house. She washed the bottles and kept them aside so she could find out what they were used for. They looked like old medicine bottles, some still had labels on, but you could barely make out what they said. It was strange how they were buried throughout the field. Mum wanted to find out about these strange items. When researching, she found that old witches' bottles would have been buried on the grounds of old properties to ward off evil spirits. This was an omen. This was the same representation of the horses' head, which they found years before when renovating the house. Maybe removing these items could have disturbed the rituals that were once conducted on the property by the previous owners. Perhaps these people were experiencing similar things to us and this is what they believed would clear the house from bad energy. This could be the reason this malevolent spirit was now roaming around the house.

As the months passed, things continued. Even though Mrs Waller was now at peace, her presence was still felt in the house. It was as if she was there in the background preventing this malevolent one from doing harm. She didn't appear to us at night anymore. But something else lay dormant in the house. It was just waiting for its time.

The autumn months soon approached, and Sharon Rectory never looked as beautiful. The rusted colours surrounded the grounds as the housed peeped through the fallen leaves. Everyone complimented my parents on their progress. They were so proud of their efforts. My Great Uncle Lawrence owned beautiful horses and asked if he could keep two in the back field for a few weeks. I loved horses and wished I could own one myself one day. Lawrence came one Saturday evening with two horses and took them to the back field which had been fenced off from the back of the house right around to the side just off the back laneway. Lawrence said, "You'll have no bother with them horses. I'll be up in the evenings to check on them." My parents were very fond of Lawrence and enjoyed his company. He loved to visit Sharon. It reminded him of his childhood; he would tell us many stories that were passed down to him.

I vaguely remember standing outside with my parents as he put the horses into the field. They seemed anxious. Maybe because it was a new environment for them. We watched as they galloped down the field until they were no longer visible. The next morning, when we came downstairs for breakfast, we looked out and saw the two horses at the front of the house. Dad was confused. "How the hell did they get out?" He went outside to try hush them back to the field. Dad, not being a real animal person struggled with the horses as he attempted to guide them into the field. It was hilarious. Once he got one in the right direction, the other one would run the opposite way. It took him over a half an hour that Sunday morning to get them back into the field. He came in scratching his head. "I don't understand how they got out. The fence is still intact, and the gates were closed."

Throughout that day the horses got out of the field several times. Dad had enough. He got Mum to ring Lawrence to figure out how they were getting out. The two horses seemed to be more content in the front garden. Every time they broke out, they went straight to the same place. Why wouldn't they stay in the back field? There was plenty of space and grass to graze on. Maybe they needed time to adjust to their new environment? That evening, Lawrence called to check on the horses, but they were nowhere to be seen. Mum explained how they broke out several times that day. We knew they just had been in the front garden five minutes prior. While searching down the back laneway we saw the two horses both in the field, content as you like. We laughed. Lawrence was so comical. "What are you on about, sir? Sure, they're in the field" Dad just shook his head with misbelief.

For as long as those two horses were at Sharon, they never stay in that back field. They would jump the fence and graze in the front garden every day. We never understood why. But I had a gut feeling something was spooking the horses. They never seemed to come up to the gate at the back laneway. I always got horrible a feeling down there, never mind the horses. Ever since I saw that 'demon dog' I never liked being there on my own. Animals always have better sixth sense than most humans. They can pick up on spirit energies before any human can. It's believed that dogs and cats have the heightened senses to otherworldly spirits. Every animal that we ever owned would somehow be affected by 'something' unseen. Mid-October, just before mid-term break, I came back from school to find out that my two beautiful Labradors ran away. They would often wander so we searched for miles around, but they were nowhere to be seen. It was as if they just vanished. I was confounded. They were my best friends. I loved the adventures I had with them. I never got over the fact they didn't ever come back. It was possible someone had taken them but even so, it was devasting for me.

In the spring of 1999, Dad began preparations to renovate the outhouses in the courtyard. He spent the evenings and weekends cleaning out the rubble and broken ruins within the sheds. The old floor on the second level needed to be removed in case it collapsed. The sheds were used for storage, but they had potential for being made into flats someday. One weekend, Dad wanted to cut the ivy on the second floor so they could start fixing the roofs of the outhouses. He climbed the wooden ladder in his tool shed onto the second level. The ivy draped through the corner of the roof and down the walls. It was extremely overgrown. He wanted to inspect how he could cut the ivy from inside. I was in the courtyard playing basketball. I watched as he walked along the hazardous floor. I could see clouds of dust fall into the lower sheds as he took steps further down the room. I stood back and shouted up to him to be careful. Within a split second the floor collapsed. I heard the echo of the falling debris collide with the ground. I ran closer, calling for

Dad. I looked into one of the glassless windows. "Dad, Dad, are you okay?"

He moaned. After a few seconds he responded, "Yes, I'm fine." I ran into the house to get Mum. Luckily there was a stack of old tractor tyres which had broken his fall. He climbed out from the rubble covered in dust. He suffered only slight cuts and bruises but was okay. His hip which he injured years before was painful but with exercise he was going to be fine. As Dad recovered, Mum remembered how Kate told us she could see someone falling from the second level when she did the walkthrough. She predicted this would happen. Kate was very accurate in her visions and this proved it. Looking back now, I can't help but think, this was the beginning of a series of unlucky events that would continue to happen over the years.

Renovations of the coachman's residence began April of 2000. This small flat adjoined to the main building beside the archway that led into the courtyard. Above the arch is a small bedroom which is used as a spare room. This is the room that was next to mine and always looked like the bed had been slept in. Dad's plan was to knock a doorway from the arch-room into the coachman's. This would give another entrance into the flat through the main house. My parents thought it would be a great space for me in the future. I was looking forward to having my own space. It meant I would have my own bathroom, kitchen and living room. But I needed the courage to move to the other end of the house on my own. It was a comfort knowing my parents were next door, but I would no longer have that when I moved into the flat.

One weekend, Dad and Grandad knocked the wall between the kitchen and sitting room to make an open-plan kitchen and living space. Dad made a beautiful cast-iron spiral staircase which fitted nicely in the corner of the kitchen. Both Mum and Dad are creative in different ways. Dad is brilliant at making things, while Mum's delicate interior finishes the job. They have great visions when set out for a project. The coachman's came along beautifully. Granddad built a beautiful redbrick fireplace surrounding an old log burner. This was the key feature for the flat. It looked so cosy and had the rustic feel to it.

Even though there was still steady activity through the house, we had gotten used to the shadows, phantom footsteps, the feeling of being watched and rumbles and movement. The eerie feel we never could shake. It still remained but wasn't yet threatening. During the coachman's renovations, the activity that we feared slowly began to happen again. Something had been disturbed. The day the door was knocked through from the coachman's, I began to hear the heavy footsteps outside my bedroom door again. It would wake me abruptly at night. It hammered loud on the landing like someone was marching outside my bedroom door. This happened a few times and I would awaken in such shock. They became louder and louder, then suddenly they would stop! This became a recurring thing. The sound would travel up the stairs, walk through the arch-room then disappear. The feeling from the staircase and arch room changed. It had a heavy feeling. It reformed once this new entranceway was made. Whatever's here has a heavier, darker presence, almost a dominant energy.

One night during the summer, this entity intended to scare me. As I lay with the covers over my head waiting for these dreaded footsteps to start, I could hear them one by one them coming up the stairs. They became louder and louder as they got closer. Once they reached the last step, there was nothing. It went dead silent… I waited for further movement as if it would pass my door into the arch-room, but after a couple of minutes there was nothing. I thought it had left. Unexpectedly, my door handle started to shake. It rattled like something was trying to enter my room. The handle vigorously shook for a few seconds, then stopped. I really thought it was someone playing a trick. Dad is a right prankster. I was positive this had to have been him. But I didn't hear anyone walk away from the door which scared me even more. The next morning, when I asked Mum what Dad was doing in the back staircase, she said, "He wasn't near those stairs last night." When I told her, she seemed shocked!

Since the renovations next door things seemed different. There was a heavier, stronger feeling in the house and nothing like when the Blue Lady was around. This may have been the horrible feeling that lingered beyond her presence but it was more profound. It was worrying. Seeing something physically move on its own without any explanation is extremely frightening. When paranormal occurrences happen and people find out, the first thing they ask is, "Why don't you run or shout or scream?" but for some people, you can't! Your body goes into a state of shock, your legs can't move, your voice doesn't work, you become numb. It's impossible for some people to understand what this is like. To be so scared that your body physically stops working from the shock. For people who experience fear to a great extent, it's almost like your heart stops or skips a beat. This entity wanted to scare me, so it could feed off my fear.

Anytime I went into the coachman's it felt extremely cold. Even if the log fire was blazing it would be freezing. Your hairs would stand on edge. Mum would often light the log fire through the day because the flat started to feel damp. At least it would circulate some heat. In the bathroom the walls felt wet with condensation. One Saturday I wanted to fight my fear. I ventured through the arch-room and into the coachman's myself. If this was going to be my new room, I needed to show what resides in here, that I wasn't afraid. When I opened the door from the arch-room and walked down the steps into the coachman's bedroom, I could smell a musty odour. It had lingered through the room. I walked down the steps into the bedroom and looked around. I stood in the middle of the room just in front of a wardrobe; two large windows looking into the courtyard were on each side. I felt like something was stopping me from going any further. This heaviness came over me. Right then, I understood what Mum felt when she couldn't walk through the kitchen door, those years previous. It was like hitting a brick wall. I started to feel the fear creep over me. I don't know what happened in that moment, it was so quick. Something grabbed my attention towards the staircase. I froze! I saw a man dangling from the banister with a noose around his neck. His eyes black and wide open. He was grey in colour. I saw him for a split second, then he was gone. This was the first time I screamed while seeing something paranormal in the years I was in the house. I was in the far end of the building, so my parents didn't hear me. I thought to myself, *Was this same spirit that rattled my door handle? Was he trying to show himself to further scare me? How can I tell anybody about this? Nobody would ever believe me.* I felt traumatised. I found it so hard to sleep after this. I would use any excuse to have a friend stay over or stay at my grandmother's in Killyverry.

Chapter IX

On the 23rd of December, my sister Victoria Lily was born. It was a quiet Christmas that year. Our house is usually the go-to place among family and friends, but it was nice to have that year just the four of us. Mum stayed at home full-time after she had Victoria. While maintaining a large house and looking after myself and a new-born, she decided it was for the best. When Victoria was three years old, she frequently spoke about a little girl called Saoirse. Since she was able to say her first full sentence, she always spoke about this young girl. We didn't know of anyone who went by this name or where Victoria heard it from. But we didn't think too much of it at the time. We assumed it must have been her imaginary friend. She often sat in the corner of the kitchen, playing with her toys as if someone was joining in with the game. One evening, when I came home from school, I sat on the ground beside

Victoria. She seemed like she was looking straight through me. Like she saw something other than me sitting there. I looked around expecting to see the same thing she saw. But there was nothing. I caught a glimpse of her yet again veering her head around me like she was following someone.

"What do you see, Victoria?"

"Saoirse," she replied.

I knew then she was seeing 'something' that looked solid to her. I knew, because I too grew up with this. I was now older and understood what was happening in the house. This was going to be the beginning of a completely different world for her.

Through most of Victoria's childhood she continued to see Saoirse. On one occasion we asked Victoria in more detail about Saoirse. What did she look like? What age was she? Where was she from? Victoria's eyes brightened up, she couldn't wait to talk to us about her friend.

As the excitement took hold, she continued to tell us, "Saoirse is wearing a brown dress with brown hair. She looks sad. She always looks sad." When we asked why Saoirse was sad, Victoria said, "Because her Mammy and Daddy is in heaven, and she misses them."

My heart sank once she told us this. Victoria walked over to the wall beside the sink in the kitchen and pointed. "This is Saoirse door home." We didn't understand what she was trying to say. There is no physical door there. It was possible Victoria was seeing some sort of gateway. Was this child a lost spirit that came through to communicate with Victoria because she knew she could see her? This didn't seem to make sense to us. However, it wasn't totally surprising given the amount of spirits Kate previously picked up during her visits to Sharon. We thought it best to get in contact with Kate again, just to see if she could explain who this young girl could be. She is our go-to person when we have any doubts or concerns regarding the spirits. We often would make jokes about Sharon Rectory being a train station for ghosts. They seem to flock to the house, maybe to receive some sort of help or communication. Or maybe they have other intentions?

Kate came to visit on a Sunday evening. She knew we had these concerns over Victoria's spirit friend. We hoped she would be able to pick up this young girl and find out why she was here. Kate sat down with Victoria and asked her to describe her friend Saoirse. As she sat with a pen and paper Victoria went on to describe her. She went into detail on what she was wearing, the way her hair was styled, just like one would see a living person. I knew Victoria wasn't making it up. While Kate sat and listened, she doodled on the piece of paper. Once they finished, Kate showed Victoria the page. Victoria shouted,

"Yes, that's Saoirse, that is just like her." Kate was able to draw the spirit child as Victoria described her.

She sat in silence for a few moments. She began picking up why this spirit child was here. "This child is trapped on the earth's plane. She can't find her parents within the spirit realm." Kate couldn't pinpoint what era this girl was from, but it wasn't in our lifetime. Kate tried to help this child find her parents. To be at peace with them. But there was obvious unfinished business here. This child had struggled to accept her death. Her story still needed to be told.

Nine years living in Sharon and being surrounded by the paranormal every day for as long as I could remember, made me question that there is a lot more to this world than we fully understand. I found it all fascinating. Yes, it can be very frightening from time to time, but seeing the remarkable communication between the living and the dead, is truly something else. How Victoria, a three-year-old child who didn't understand anything about what she was seeing or experiencing, talked to us about this young spirit girl. Describing things that weren't to our knowledge, only to have it confirmed through someone we considered to be very reliable. I have always had my doubts about what I saw when I was growing up, even though it was actually happening to me. Sometimes our brain can't accept anything other than a logical explanation or reason. Everything I had seen, heard and felt before

Victoria was born, was extremely remarkable but I never looked at it in any other way than being "a scary and horrible situation." I wanted to learn more about why I saw ghosts and what makes them want to communicate with me. I began to embrace the spirit world and see it as a gift. It was clear from previous experiences that some of these spirits mean no harm. It is simply their way of connecting and commentating with us. It is the other entities, the nasty and malevolent ones that we need to watch. But how could something that wasn't visible to the naked eye have total control over your physical being? This was something I didn't think possible or in any way would happen to me. This was going to be a learning curve for not only me, but other members in my family.

In the summer of 2005, I made the decision to move into the most active part of the house. And yes, most people would ask, "Why they hell would you do that?" But I wanted to face my fears. What resided in the coachman's wasn't going to control me. I wouldn't say I wanted to challenge 'it', but I wasn't going to let it scare me out of my home. Little did I know what would lay ahead for me as I braved the nasty one over time.

Victoria was getting older and she needed her own bedroom. My old room was ideal. It was right next to my parents' room, so it was perfect for as she got older. Slowly I started to move my things bit by bit into the arch-room. I wanted to test the waters in here first. Just to see how it felt being at the other side of the house on my own. This was a much smaller room with a toilet and sink in the corner. It was cosy, but had an eerie feeling linked within it. The first week I couldn't really sleep. I had been so used to my old bedroom and having moved into a smaller room it felt like the walls were closing in on me. It even happened when my eyes were closed. I don't know if it was the energy in the room that whirled around me or if it was my mind playing tricks. But whatever it was, it continued to happen.

My time spent in the arch-room was bearable. Surprisingly! I sometimes felt a swaying feeling in the room, but I wasn't sure why it happened. It felt like I was on a boat. I would still hear the footsteps coming up the back staircase at night, but it seemed to only happen on certain occasions. I'm unsure why this was. Maybe it became weak because I didn't show the fear I once did? I felt I showed more bravery in the house since I moved into this room. I wasn't a child anymore and I didn't let the horrible spirits bully me into fearing them. I felt I had more control over my fear. Yes, I still got scared from time to time but it was nothing compared to what I once was. I still heard the knocks and bangs and sometimes heard chattering or whispers within the coachman's. This would be frightening. I could never make out what they were saying. It was like two people having a constant conversation. It would sometimes keep me awake at night. It did put me off moving into the coachman's at first but, I couldn't stay in the arch-room any longer.

Before I knew it two years had passed, and I wanted to bite the bullet and move in next door. I didn't intend to stay that long in the arch-room. I wanted to move into the coachman's shortly after moving from the other room, but it was as if something kept stopping me.

The end of August 2007, I moved next door. I started college a week later. I wanted to be in before starting so I could organise the space and have a desk and area for studying. My first night was strange; the layout of the room was different. It wasn't just a square room. It had hidden corners, which I didn't like, and the spiral staircase which I saw the grey man hanging from. I felt okay in the arch bedroom because it was small and still was part of the main house. At least I didn't feel miles apart from my parents. But across that threshold into the coachman's, it felt like a whole other house. In the other bedrooms I would keep a light on throughout the night so I could see each corner, but in here I couldn't. I feared for what lurked around the corners. I felt whatever walked slowly up the back staircase at night, was now in here with me. I didn't feel it in the arch-room. This felt like a different energy. I felt more of a female presence when I stayed in there. It wasn't as pleasant as Mrs Waller but wasn't bad either. Since I moved, I started to feel the fear again. I knew by fearing this thing it would use it against me. This was an intelligent spirit. If it even was a spirit. It knew I was feeling vulnerable, doubting myself for moving here. I could sense it around me when I sat in the room. I would lay in the bed awake looking around me. I kept the bathroom light on so it would shine through into the bedroom. I always needed the light. I never slept in the total darkness at Sharon. The darkness there terrifies me. Although, keeping the light on probably made things a little worse. You were more inclined to see movements from the shadows when there was a slight bit of light. I would tend to get a glimpse of them out the corner of my eye. Maybe in total darkness I wouldn't see them? But I didn't know if I was brave enough to try it.

One night I got up and turned off the bathroom light. I lay back down with the room in complete blackness. My other senses began to kick in. I felt I could hear a pin drop. I pulled the covers over my head, regretting the decision of sleeping in the dark. But I was too scared to move again. I never moved all night. I just lay there, half asleep with the covers over my head. I thought, *If I can get through this first night in darkness, I can manage the rest.* After a couple of hours, I woke to hear a rustling sound somewhere in the room.

It sounded like it came from the door that led into the main house. The rustling noise moved down the steps into the room, right to the end of my bed. Then the noise stopped. I was so scared. I didn't want to look up. I dreaded to think what could have been there. I kept thinking over and over in my head, *What if I sit up to look and the grey man is standing there looking back at me?* I slept so lightly that night. As morning drew, the room started to get brighter. That was the only time I got sleep. I felt safer knowing it was daylight outside. I did ask myself, *Why did I move in here?* but I needed to prove to myself I could do this. I didn't want to live in fear for as long as I was in Sharon.

The first few weeks were hard. I was ready to admit defeat and move back into the arch bedroom. But something wouldn't let me. I still wanted to face my fears and prove to myself and whatever resided in there that I could overpower it. I continued to hear the shuffling of clothes at night and I wasn't falling asleep any better. I started to feel my energy drain from being in the room. Going to college was a break, even though I was so exhausted. I was studying Health and Social Studies and between my work placements and assignments, I kept busy. My parents still had the reoccurring paranormal events in the main house. They often heard the piano playing by itself in the main living room. The shutter for the keys would always be closed and the piano wasn't tuned in, but the sound of a light melody still played throughout the house. The main house haunting never felt as threating. It was mostly playful or residual. My parents for the first time in years felt like they could live with the spirits. I, on the other hand, never felt more threatened. I felt like whatever was in the coachman's wasn't leaving. Its presence just grew stronger as time went on, but I still couldn't leave. I wasn't sure if it wanted to keep me there or if it was just my ignorance to sit on until I was made to move.

As the winter set in, I started to feel my health deteriorate. I always felt tired and was physically sick. I didn't know if it was the mountain of college work or because I wasn't sleeping through the night. But it was beginning to have an effect on me. On my days off, I spent most of the day in bed. I was starting to fall into a deep depression. I knew my parents thought it was the pressure from my college work but looking back now, I don't think it was. I always felt fine when I was in school, it changed as soon as I came home. It would suddenly it hit me as I entered over that threshold. When going in the room it was like something sucked the remaining energy from me. But then, I didn't accept it was anything paranormal. I started to grow so angry towards everyone. I would snap at Mum and Victoria or anyone who crossed me. I was losing myself! I felt hatred towards people I didn't even know. Anyone who entered the coachman's could instantly feel the difference in atmosphere compared to the main house. Because I was living in there, I didn't feel it anymore. This was my environment and people weren't allowed unless I welcomed them. I was angry with the world. I thought I was past the whole moody teenager thing, but this was much more. I couldn't explain why I felt this way.

Chapter X

In the spring of 2009, I focused on freshly painting and decorating the kitchen/living area downstairs. I wanted more of my own independence. I wanted to cook my own dinners and be in my own living area. I just wanted my *own* company. I was starting to isolate myself from my family and friends. I don't know why. I just felt like everything annoyed me. One evening while I was in the bathroom, I felt like there were eyes on me. I know this might sound ridiculous, but it felt like there were eyes looking at me through the tiled wall. I started to feel uncomfortable. Even showering became difficult because I always felt watched. I didn't think this presence could get any stronger, but it did. It was nothing like I had ever experienced before in the house. This felt dark.

I woke one morning to go to college and noticed strange marks on my legs. They looked like bite marks. They just appeared from nowhere. You could clearly see four teeth marks on the top and six on the bottom, it was visible just above my knee on one leg and on my lower thigh on the other. It didn't look like any sort of animal's bites. I never felt anything bite me through the night and I would have woken if I did. I was confused as to what it was. At this stage I still didn't believe this was anything paranormal. *How could a ghost leave a physical mark on me?* I went on to college as normal that day, putting it to the back of my mind. I was in my final year of the course and I needed to focus on my studies to get me into my nursing degree. I was under so much pressure. I blamed it on my exams and stress that I was feeling like this. I was past fearing the spirits at this stage. I honestly had no time to think about the bites. But I wish I had. I just wish I had looked into why these marks appeared on me. Or at least stopped to think what could have caused it.

There was one module in the course that I took a keen interest in. 'Complementary therapy' was my favourite subject. It fascinated me how a wide range of western medicines and techniques were used to help people with illnesses and diseases. I wanted to learn one of these therapies. I didn't know which, but I knew this what I was meant to do. By chance, I found a woman who ran daily workshops on Reiki Healing. I read up on the healing and found it fascinating. I booked myself into the workshop the next day. I didn't really know what to expect or how it worked, but I was open to trying something new. There didn't seem to be many people, only four or five attended. I couldn't help to think, *What a bad turnout.* How was it even worth this woman's while running the workshop for such a small group? As she introduced herself, she asked us one by one our names and why we decided to attend the workshop. I was nervous. I knew this healing was all about working with energy, I was somewhat drawn to do this. I'm not sure why but I felt like I was meant to do this. Maybe I was meant to help myself heal before helping other people. I explained how I came across the module in college and Reiki seemed to stand out as a therapy I wanted to try. It was nice being among a small group of people. It felt comfortable. The first hour we focused on the therapy and how it worked, then the lady explained how we needed to be attuned with the healing. I didn't know what this meant or entailed but I was intrigued.

She sat us down in the middle of a circle one by one. We sat with our eyes closed; the lady continued to do some sort of movement above our heads. I could feel a ball of energy circulate inside me, around me, all over me. It was like nothing I have ever felt before. It was warm, refreshing and enlightening. I came away feeling like a completely different person. I didn't feel as exhausted, fatigued or depressed. Maybe there was something to this Reiki Healing therapy? On my way home, I felt great. But as soon as I walked into the door of the main house, something felt different. I felt something had crawled over me. I had never felt like this before. It was like walking into a large spider's web, with a thousand spiders crawling all over me. I walked towards the bottom bedroom and down to the back staircase. As soon as I crossed the threshold to go up the stairs, it felt like there was something watching me. It was strange. I remember walking up the stairs shaking my arms and head convinced there was a spider's web stuck on me. When I got to my room I couldn't wait to check in the mirror if there was something on me. But nothing! Why did I feel this?

That night, as I got ready for bed, the bathroom felt a lot colder than normal. The whole place felt weird. It felt like I was in somebody else's house. As I looked into the bathroom mirror, I thought I glimpsed a face coming through the wall behind me. I looked around quickly, but nothing! I didn't want to think on what I saw. I was scaring myself. I know this sounds silly, but it felt like the wall had eyes watching me. I kept the light of the bathroom on and I jumped into bed. I drifted off to sleep really easily after this. Around half two or three that morning I woke with such a bang in the bedroom. It sounded like something fell with force. Like something had been thrown from across the room. I jumped up, expecting to find something laying on the floor. But there was nothing. Everything was still in place from what I could see. I lay back down, I could feel my heart beating fast in my chest. It gave me such a fright. I struggled to get back to sleep. I drifted off for a few minutes then woke again. This happened many times at morning. What happened to me next changed my perspective of Sharon Rectory. I remember opening my eyes and as I woke, my heart started to race from fear. What I saw standing at the end of my bed was nothing like I had ever seen or will ever see again. As I pulled the bedcovers back, I saw this tall, black figure standing in the middle of the room watching me as I lay in bed. It was over seven feet tall. It was solid black and felt extremely negative. I could just make out the head and shoulders. Its body ran straight down from its shoulders. There was no real shape, just a head, shoulders and straight body. My heart instantly stopped. I couldn't breathe. I felt like I was suffocating for what felt like hours. But within a moment I took a deep breath and shot up in the bed. *What the hell was that?* I looked around the room. But it was gone. Had this 'thing' finally shown itself? I didn't know how to feel about this. *Did I really see it, or had I mistaken it for the shadow of something in the room? Maybe it was a nightmare and I just remember waking up from it? It felt so real, so it couldn't have been.*

I really questioned my belief in what I just saw. But I remember seeing it so clearly. I was scared. I didn't know what I was up against; it had to have been nasty. The negative feeling that lingered, made me feel sick. *Where did this thing come from?* This definitely wasn't like the other manifestations I'd seen. I needed my guard up for this one.

I started to see strange things more frequently after this. Not only in Sharon Rectory, but anywhere I went. I felt this difference after the Reiki workshop. It was like it opened me more to the spirit world. I wouldn't say I became a psychic medium overnight, but I became more sensitive to the energies around me. When I was in the house, I always felt like I was being watched and the unexplainable cold spots, even when the heating was on, but after this I saw everything differently. I felt like there was a darkness in certain rooms. What I mean by darkness, I feel like when looking at the library, it had a darker appearance to it, compared to the large sitting room. It was like I could sense something depraved happened there. Most days when I walk past the dining room, I glimpsed people moving in the corner of my eye. It always feels busy in the dining room and kitchen area. Like there is a rush of energy moving between these rooms. I understood what Kate meant all those years ago when she first visited Sharon. Sometimes I am convinced that it's

Mum, Dad or Victoria moving between rooms, but I could be alone when it happens.

I was becoming more aware of the spirits that walked in the house. I learned from then how to sense the different types of energies. From the good to the bad. I knew from the main house to the coachman's how different it felt. It was like positive to negative, but some days it felt stronger. I felt I could understand what Kate was feeling when she walked through the house, but maybe not as strong of a sense as she did. It all started to make sense. I knew that the shadow person I had seen that night was real. And it wasn't good, but it was there. This entity had been making me really sick for months. My anger, depression and fatigue were all linked to this unhinged spirit. But how could I stop it? I wanted to learn about this, to study more about the paranormal. I wanted to piece the puzzle together of Sharon Rectory's unnerving history. To link these spirits to the times they once lived. This is where my journey really began.

Now that I realised what I was facing in the coachman's, I did fear it. I knew 'it' wanted my energy. This is what it fed off. My fear! I called it 'it' as I didn't yet know what it was or where it came from. It didn't belong to this house. It made the coachman's feel different compared to the main house. I don't believe it was the same spirit that walked the back staircase during most of my childhood. I was scared of those footsteps, but I didn't feel the threat that I felt with this one. The spirit of the back staircase never made me feel sick, drained or depressed. That's how I established the negative one from the rest of the spirits. When 'they' mean physical and mental harm, they are negative. I knew this was attacking me. I occasionally woke with physical marks on my body. Ones that I couldn't explain. I was in a relationship, which ended abruptly. I felt this may have played a part in my thoughts towards this person. My personality changed towards him. I felt I didn't have control. When that relationship ended, I still felt like this. My personality switched. Sometimes I wouldn't even remember doing things or saying things which insulted or hurt someone. I knew my parents didn't understand. It is only when I look back now, I know this negative one played a large part in it all.

Late 2009 renovations of the outer house roofs began. The roofs were stripped bare for reconstruction to start early the following year. The corner of the coachman's ridge was opened, which left only the attic space ceiling and a sheet of strong plastic between the outside and my bedroom. I didn't want to move rooms during this time. And I don't really know why. Maybe something had prevented me from leaving the coachman's. Maybe because 'it' had that constant fix of energy and mental hold over me. I never really put in much thought until looking back at what went on.

Christmas was around the corner and I won't lie, the coachman's was freezing cold. Even with the heating on and fire lit, I still needed an electric fan heater to use in the mornings. As Christmas morning soon approached, I abruptly woke around 6.30am with a strange noise in the room. When I looked up to check, I noticed my electric fan heater had turned itself on. My heart was in my throat! I knew I had unplugged the extension lead out of the wall before going to bed. I was terrified! I watched it as it speeded up to the highest setting before stopping seconds later. I was not willing to get up and switch it off. I just lay there in shock watching it as it turned. I knew I wasn't going to be able to go back to sleep after seeing that. It was still dark outside, and I didn't want to get up. I just lay there, with the covers over my head. I wanted to wait until the sun came up before making my way downstairs. A couple of hours passed and it felt like it was days. I got up and walked over to the heater. I already knew the plug had been pulled out, but I needed to confirm for my own sanity. I couldn't explain it. I'd had this heater for months and that never happened before. I still have the same fan heater to this day, and yet it has never done this again. When I told my parents, they couldn't help but laugh. Dad sarcastically said, "Maybe the ghosts thought you were cold?" He knew he had to make light of the moment because it had scared me. What else was it capable of doing? Between moving objects, turning on and off electrical appliances, mental and physical attacks? When was it going to stop?

A new year had come, and I thought this to be a new chapter in my life. I wanted to make the most out of a bad situation. I loved to go out and have fun with my friends. I would throw get-togethers at mine before heading into town for a night out. I knew that if we had pre-drinks at mine, I could invite the girls to come back and stay. I really wanted the company. I didn't want to say that I felt scared living in the coachman's or let them to know just how bad things felt while living there. They would never stay if they knew the stuff that was happening. On one occasion, when a close friend stayed for the night, she woke in terror as she felt something hold her down in the bed. She froze! She couldn't move with such pressure holding her down. As she tried to reach over to wake me, her arms felt heavy. Like something was stopping her from getting help. She couldn't scream although she was screaming inside. When she felt the pressure release, she woke me in an absolute panic. As she told me what had happened, I knew straight away it was this 'thing' making itself known to her. Showing her just how strong it was. She said it was the most terrifying thing she had experienced.

This has been a common occurrence within

Sharon since I can remember. I believe the correct term is sleep paralysis, but many times this has happened when we were wide awake. I believe the spirits like to show such strengths, maybe so they can show what they are capable of.

Chapter XI

Four years passed since I first moved into the coachman's and the first day was a distant memory. I met Gabriel, in January of 2011. With his logical way of thinking, he found it extremely difficult to believe our experiences. He lived locally, just a short drive from Sharon Rectory. He had heard the stories of Sharon but didn't believe them. My dad would regularly joke about the 'ghosts' within the house to Gabriel, but he would think there was a rational reason behind everything. After a few months Gabriel moved in with me. We rarely spent time apart. I felt safe when he was there. But the activity didn't stop. The coachman's still held this negative identity within it.

In August 2011, I became extremely depressed. I had hit my lowest. I struggled to interact with anyone. I seemed to have pushed everyone that I cared for away. I spent the whole time in the coachman's, locking myself away from the world. I had been struggling for years with extreme fatigue and sleepless nights. My doctor prescribed me sleeping pills in hopes of getting me into a better sleeping pattern so I wouldn't feel the fatigue effects during the day. How was I to tell my doctor the reason for not sleeping? Or why I felt sick and drained all the time? I couldn't say, "My house is haunted, and an evil spirit is attacking me." I would have been admitted straight to the psych ward. It was so hard to tell anyone why I was feeling this way. Who would believe me? It was hard growing up in a haunted house, dealing with people laughing at us, starting rumours about my family, saying we were on drugs and were hallucinating or seeking attention. My parents found it hard to believe that there was anything evil in the house. They thought the spirits were just the mislaid souls of the ones that lost their life to an awful double murder. Trapped within the walls of Sharon for all eternity. But I knew that I felt something evil.

Late one Friday night in mid-November, I sat alone downstairs in the coachman's watching TV. I don't know what came over me, nor do I remember much of what happened. All I recall is going upstairs, taking the sleeping pills out of the container and taking them one by one. I can't remember much after that. I woke up in A&E with Mum beside me, worried about what I had done. It pains me talking about what happened that night. Many people didn't know what I had done or why. How would anyone ever understand? There was no obvious reason for why I felt so depressed. I had been going through a stressful time indeed, but it was nothing that couldn't be fixed. Was there a possibility this entity made me do it? Or was it living in such an oppressive space for many years which drove me to the point of suicide? I knew from this point the coachman's was dangerous for me, but I had nowhere else to go. I needed to learn how to protect myself from what was in there. I was leaving myself open for these attacks and I needed to close myself off. If there ever was a time where I could use the term 'to fight my demons' this was it. I needed to get back into my own way of thinking again and not let this 'thing' bring me down. I was suffering badly with depression, but I sought the help of a counsellor and soon was able to get myself back on track.

Kate got in contact with Mum and asked if we were interested in joining a psychic development class. This would help us understand more of the spirit world and it couldn't have come at a better time. I knew this would help me understand what was going on. Maybe I could identify what I was dealing with by my new knowledge from the group. This would be the start of a new and interesting path for myself and Mum. When we joined the group, some of the members knew about our current ghostly experiences. Curious and intrigued, they wanted to know more. We talked about the murders that took place over two hundred years ago and what we experienced daily. They were all fascinated and couldn't wait to visit the house. They wanted to feel and experience these spirits for themselves. We met with the group once a week. I felt somewhat at ease with them. They all had their own ghostly experiences, which was a breath of fresh air. They knew and understood what we were going through. Maybe not to the same extent but they had seen and felt unexplainable things in their life. It felt normal talking with them. Not to be judged or classed as 'insane' talking about 'ghosts', but we didn't only talk about everything haunted. It was enlightening to hang with people who got you and had the same things in common. The most important aspect we would learn in the group was to protect and ground ourselves, especially when interacting with spirits. Each person's experiences and senses are different to the next. Some people are more open than others and may be able to hear or see a spirit clearer.

A couple of months had passed, and I felt I understood slightly more about the spirit world. Kate was a great supporter and teacher as well as the other ladies and gentlemen in the group. We arranged visits with them to come to Sharon to see what they thought. A few had an instant connection to the house, like they had been pulled there. That tends to happen a lot, even in the present time. It could well be from a past connection in another life or maybe a spirit was drawn to a certain person. Each person that visits who is sensitive, can pick up relatable things to us or the history of the house. As Mum and I were becoming more attuned, she started to see more spirits within the house also. It was like an awaking to her. It now wasn't only Mrs Waller's spirit that she could see but that of others. Both she and Mrs Waller had a strong bond. They are both the ladies of Sharon Rectory. Even though Mrs Waller is at peace, her presence still lingers. Looking back now and even to this date, I think they were exactly the same. Apparently, Mrs Waller was house proud. She had a particular way of decorating, with soft furnishings and knick-knacks; each one had a place. Mum is the very same. You often see her walking around the house fixing or moving things. She feels as though when she moves a certain item, she gets the sense it wasn't meant to be there. Could this be Mrs Waller telling her it's meant to be in a different place?

We continued to meet once a week for our psychic development class; it helped that we all had a close connection. All our experiences soon interlinked. It was strange, I could never explain it, but Mum seemed to have the strongest connection within the group. Her experiences outside soon showed this.

One that was most peculiar happened late one night, while Mum fell into a deep sleep. She saw herself standing in the middle of the kitchen. She didn't know how she got there. It was as though she was astral travelling. The door which led into the back kitchen was opened, and she stood looking toward the back door as though she was waiting for someone to walk in. Instantly, an old woman entered from the back door and the kitchen. She wore a long, woven skirt which fell below her knees. Her hair was wispy and swept around her wrinkled old face. She slowly began to walk towards the main kitchen. Mum could sense this woman was pure evil. She began to shout at her, telling her, "GET OUT! GET OUT! GET OUT!" The woman laughed as she walked closer to her. Mum started to show her anger and continued to chase the woman out of the house. She woke from the dream still shouting, "GET OUT!" She felt like she was under attack from this woman. To her it felt so real. She was completely confused as to what had happened. Who was this woman and why she was in her dream? Mum didn't feel like she was linked to Sharon Rectory or the grounds. This felt like a malevolent, sinister entity that was trying to get to her through her dreams. It was too vivid to be just a 'normal' dream. Little did she know this woman had shown herself to two of the ladies from the psychic development class just days after Mum's dream.

A week later, we met up with the class as normal. Mum told everyone about this strange woman who came to her in a dream. She continued to describe what this woman wore, how she looked and the general feel she got from her. But things got stranger. Not only did Mum have this awful experience, two of the ladies from the group also had the same interaction with this old woman. One woke to the same woman coming out of the mirror in her bedroom. She sat up in the bed and watched as this woman stepped out of a long mirror from the other end of her room and walked towards her bed. She completely froze, but within moments she had gone. She wore the exact clothes that Mum described and felt the same malevolent energy from her. The other woman in the group also experienced this old lady at night. She too woke to feel somebody lay in the bed beside her. Given that this woman lives alone, it completely scared her to her inner core. She woke to feel the body of a person lying beside her. As she slowly turned in the bed dreading to see what it was, she caught a glimpse of this old woman lying beside her. But before she could react, she was gone. I was so glad that I hadn't witnessed such a traumatic experience as this. The three ladies described this 'woman' the same and felt similar negative, sinister feelings from her.

When researching further on the meaning of this entity, it shows that it was possibly 'the night hag' or 'old hag' that each of the ladies perceived. This could have been a test to show their strengths in psychic development. When opening yourself to the spirit world you need to be able to deal with not only lost souls of loved ones but negative spirits also. Understanding that not every encounter with spirits is pleasant, but how to mentally cope when we you face these adverse entities.

Gabriel and I were having our ups and downs. Maybe it was because he didn't understand just how much living in the coachman's was affecting me. It was hard to explain what was causing the depression, especially when he wasn't open to believe it. Gabriel was very sceptical over our experiences and even though he stayed from time to time, he still thought it was all nonsense. This caused friction in our relationship. When unexplainable things occurred while he was there, I'd tell him these were the things that happened on a regular basis. He would argue with me to stop blaming it on the paranormal. I had lived with this for over 16 years, yet he would still fight me over how ridiculous it sounded.

As months passed, Gabriel woke one night trembling in fear. I had never seen him react like this before. I didn't know what had happened, so I started to panic. His forehead was dripping wet and he seemed to be hyperventilating. Once he caught his breath, he said something had held him down in the bed. He explained it exactly how my friend did. He didn't see what it was, but knew the pressure was of something forcefully holding him down. When this happens, its intention is to scare. It seems to gain strength with fear. Things would happen more on a regular basis when we felt such terror. Even after Gabriel's first experience, he stood strongly on the argument of "there is an explanation for what happened."

In September 2012 I had my first son, Noah. Leading up to his birth, I was very physically and mentally drained. Being in such an oppressive environment, I struggled more with my pregnancy. I was hospitalised for a short time due to severe dehydration and sickness. Even though this wasn't due to anything paranormal, it could have played a small role. After I had Noah, the sickness continued. Months were going by fast and I felt my energy was constantly zapped. The pattern arose again where I struggled to leave the coachman's. I felt that draw to come back once I left. I would stay in bed until late afternoon struggling to tend to Noah. Even though Noah was a good baby and sleep great at night, I felt like I was constantly sick. It had got to the point where Mum would fight with me most days, making me get up and leave the house. I wouldn't say I was suffering from depression but more so physical exhaustion. Noah's cot sat at the bottom of my bed and often he would gaze around him as though he could see someone other than me. It reminded me of how Victoria was when she was a baby. Following something with their eyes when nothing was physically there. Noah would become fixated on 'something' that was unseen to me. I knew this was him seeing the spirits. I wasn't scared so much for him in the main building, but I feared him being in the coachman's. We had no choice but to stay there and save so we could afford a place of our own. When Noah was slightly older, I moved his cot into the arch bedroom which was right next door from the coachman's. After this move Noah became very unsettled. I put it down to him being in new surroundings and thought he would settle within the week. Most nights I would sit in the arch bedroom doorway, listening to him scream, crying, hoping and praying he would fall asleep. As most mothers know, when their child cries, they automatically know why they are crying. May it be hunger, fear or pain. Noah's cry seemed to be a scared cry. I knew something had to have been scaring him. I would sometimes need to stay beside him on the floor near his cot to get him to sleep. This continued for weeks. It got to the point where I needed to look for another place to live. I couldn't let this 'thing' scare my son too.

A few weeks had passed; me, Gabriel and Noah moved from Sharon and rented a house about 10-minute drive from home. I won't lie, it was good to finally be out of the coachman's. To live somewhere that didn't scare me or make me feel mentally and physically drained, was such a joy. For once I felt 'normal'. For the first time since I could remember I didn't see things in my own home. I made this space my own for myself and my family. I wanted to save Noah from seeing the things that scared me as an adult, never mind a child. I, myself, was only learning now how to cope with it all. At least until I knew I was strong enough to protect my family from these energies 'good' as well as 'bad'. Even though the spirits that meant no harm were around, they still would physically drain me of my energy. Now they could get our attention, it seemed bad for us. They would continue to toy, especially when you least expected it. Spirits can be mischievous, especially children spirits. Items would randomly disappear from time to time but turn up in a completely different place than where we first left it. When I left home, the things continued to scare Mum and Victoria. It was as if whatever picked on me started to terrorise them. Victoria was very opened and struggled to filter them out. It was like history repeating itself, she continued to lay awake through the night waiting to hear the sound of these footsteps step by step coming up from the back staircase and stop outside her bedroom. When Dad travelled out of the country for work, Victoria would stay in with Mum most nights as they felt safer in pairs.

Chapter XII

As though it seemed to be a pattern for activity to heighten at night, Mum continued to experience on and off encounters with new spirits. It appeared that she would know if the spirits were linked to the house or not. She was developing quicker than the rest of us psychically and would occasionally feel emotions of the spirits before they passed on. She could walk into a room within the house and feel completely overwhelmed with emotions for no reason. It got to the point where she had to control and filter these emotions and allow them to resurface when it was most relevant to the situation. She didn't want them to overtake her body without permission. This was showing her empathic abilities. Which is an amazing experience when controlled in a grounded and safe environment. I too began to develop my empathic capabilities. I not only felt the pain and suffering of spirits, but the living people around me. It really began to take its toll on me physically and in my job caring for people, I could almost feel the pain they too would suffer. I know this sounds too farfetched and unbelievable to some folk, but to me it wasn't. After what I lived with from the supernatural world, nothing was too much of a shock to me anymore. I had experienced and seen so much already, and this was only a few years into my understanding and journey with the paranormal.

Victoria was getting older and was becoming very intuitive with her spiritual surroundings. Being born and brought into an unusual situation surrounding the paranormal, it was only time before she too would develop these same abilities. She often saw these spirits within the house. She could even hear them talk to her. Like they were at the other end of a phone call having a conversation. She would often tell Mum what they would tell her. Out of all the spirits, there was one particularly that Victoria continued to have a connection with. This was the spirit of the young girl, Saoirse. Like Mum had done with me, she never encouraged Victoria with the spirits. She would reassure that the spirits she was seeing were not a threat to her and that she saw them too. It wasn't the right time for Victoria to know the evil that lurks within Sharon. But she knew she couldn't stop Victoria from seeing such things. This was a gift, but it was also a curse. It was going to be Victoria's decision whether or not she wanted to block them out or embrace them and learn how to ground and protect herself. In time, Victoria would make this decision.

One weekend, during Victoria's mid-term holidays, she asked Mum if she could stay at a friend's house for a sleepover. Dad had been out of the country for work and Mum usually didn't like staying in the house alone. But she didn't want Victoria missing out. She would sooner put Victoria and myself first and risk being alone in the house, than force us to stay with her. But this night, something happened that shook her to the core. After she dropped Victoria at her friend's and drove home, reluctant towards what lay ahead, she came in and did what she usually does most nights. She watched TV in the kitchen for a couple of hours before going to bed. She didn't feel in any way different in the house or sense anything out of the ordinary. When she got into bed, she put all the unnerving thoughts to the back of her mind. She struggled to fall asleep, so she turned the TV on. Just so there was background noise until she drifted off. After a couple of hours, she woke to a weird sensation of something hitting her in the legs. She dreaded to look up. She knew no one else was in the house, so what was this 'thing' hitting her above the bedsheets. The fear creeped over her. She slowly pulled the covers down from her face and peeked her head over. She saw a young girl standing at the bottom of the bed.

Directly on top of her legs. She described her as though she was doing somersaults, hitting her in the leg as she looped around and around. Mum tried to shout but no words would come out. The girl looked grey in colour. She had long black hair which fell around her face and she was probably was aged between 7 and 9 years. She wore a long, old-fashioned, white nightdress. Mum couldn't believe what she was seeing. This wasn't a dream. She was wide awake!

The girl looked to be saying something, but Mum couldn't understand. She talked as though something had happened to her mouth. She couldn't hear the words as such, just a mumble. Each time Mum tried to shout, talk or communicate in any way, she felt as though the 'cat had her tongue'. What was this girl trying to do? Mum couldn't help but think was this the young girl Victoria had previously talked about. She couldn't remember Victoria saying anything about her mouth being like that. What felt like hours to Mum was only a few minutes in real time. The spirit girl had gone, and Mum sat up in the bed in complete shock. She worried about the intentions this spirit had towards her. Why show herself now and not years previous? This was the first time she had ever witnessed this young girl and it wouldn't be her last.

The following day Mum rang to tell me what happened. She made it clear this wasn't a dream. There was a reason she came to her. She needed to tell her something but couldn't. Mum knew this girl had something to do with the house, but she couldn't put her finger on it. Something didn't add up. We knew there was at least 100 years of missing history that we didn't know of. Could this girl be linked to those lost years? We only ever knew of the main events that happened in the late 1700s and the recent tragedy in the last 70 years, and they were all documented. This was going to be the beginning of another piece to a large puzzle. During our next get-together for the psychic development class, Mum told everyone the experience she had with this young girl. We thought it best that they organised to come to Sharon and see what they felt. This girl seemed to seek help and we hoped that within the group she could maybe gather her energy from us to communicate.

In the meantime, a family friend happened to be working with an elderly man that was familiar to the townland of Newtowncunningham. In conversation, he asked if she knew of an old house called Sharon Rectory. Shocked, she replied that she knew the current owners. He continued to tell her how in the 50s he read in the local newspaper, two young women had seen the ghost of a young girl while they stayed a night in the house. Apparently, this young girl was supposed to be buried under the kitchen floor. While Mum's friend couldn't wait to ring and tell her, she was oblivious as to what Mum experienced just a few nights prior. This was all starting to make sense. Could this girl only be showing herself to Mum now because she knew she had the ability to help? We didn't know the exact date in the 50s that this was supposedly published or what newspaper it was, but it was a starting point to our research. We went to the local library in search of the archives hoping to strike luck, but with even a year, it wasn't narrowing it down. This was like finding a needle in a haystack. I felt we were giving up hope. It was going to be impossible to help this girl find peace if we didn't know what happened her.

On the evening the class came to Sharon; everyone had their own capabilities and skills in communicating or sensing spirits. But one lady in particular was great at communicating with spirits. She was clairvoyant as well as audiovoyant. This meant she saw and heard the spirits clearly. As soon as she walked in, it was like a sensory overload. The way she described the house, it was like a train station for ghosts. There were many that seemed to be linked with the house. Some had unfinished business and weren't ready to leave. But our main focus then was to find out more about this young girl. She clearly wanted to tell Mum something, but for some reason couldn't. This group was the only hope we had to find out what we could do to help.

We walked through the house, just so each person could feel and sense the surroundings. Again, the one lady continued to pick up everything. She suddenly said, "I'm not where you think, I'm buried!" She continued to walk towards the reception hallway. She turned right and stopped at the cellar door, we followed. She appeared to be guided by something. If it was the spirit of the little girl, we didn't know as of yet. We just followed as she felt the pull to this area of the house. She opened the cellar door and began to walk down the stairs. She turned and stopped for a moment before continuing down the cellar corridor. She continued to the end but felt as though she needed to go further back. "This wall wasn't always here!" she said. We knew from my grandfather that tunnels used to run from under the house, but we weren't sure where to. She was convinced that something was behind the wall. She said that this little girl's body was behind this wall. We all looked in complete shock. This couldn't be. Surely, if a young girl had gone missing all those years ago, there would have been some kind of investigation under the circumstances. But then again, if she was an orphan and if this happened centuries ago, would anyone have gone looking otherwise? This was all new to us.

We had never heard of any other deaths or murders that took place in the house because we couldn't find the documentation. The question being, was every possible death on the land documented? This was something we couldn't yet answer. There is a lot of history yet to uncover that we still don't know about. So, anything is possible. This spirit girl continued to psychically communicate through this lady. She said, "A man cut out my tongue!" All of a sudden, the penny dropped. This was why Mum couldn't understand her when she appeared and why she too felt like something was wrong with her mouth. Things were starting to add up. We tried to get more. She continued, "He hurt me, he cut out my tongue and buried me alive behind the wall." This was a big statement, but it was too relevant to what we currently experienced. To me, any of this was possible but until further proof, it remains a mystery. Either way we had made leeway on the unknown of this young girl. It was something we could further research to maybe link a date or name or something that could back this up. What we now knew from the session was that this young girl, possibly an orphan, who once had a connection in the house, was assaulted and abused by a man, then buried alive behind the cellar wall. If we only knew what year this wall was built that blocked the entranceway to the tunnels, we could narrow down the search. This was now another mysterious death that occurred within Sharon's walls.

Late August 2013, Mum received a phone call from a Northern Ireland paranormal team, asking if they could conduct an investigation into the haunting of Sharon Rectory. They continued to explain how they had heard about our experiences and found it extremely interesting. They wanted to see and feel this for themselves. We knew that the local people heard of our on-going experiences, but it was a surprise when an actual paranormal team wanted to witness this for themselves. I am such a big fan of paranormal TV shows and I was shocked when Mum told me there was one that wanted to conduct an investigation right in our home. But a part of me had a bad feeling about this. Could this wreak havoc with the spirits in Sharon? I knew the team wouldn't be able to rid the house of spirits, not even a blessing from a priest could do it! Unless it was the actual Ghostbusters I didn't have much hope for the house ever being anything 'normal'. The spirits clearly wanted us to know this was 'their' home and they weren't leaving!

A few weeks later the paranormal team arrived to investigate. This would be the first EVER paranormal investigation to be held within Sharon Rectory. It was an honour to be a part of this history, but I was really nervous! I didn't know what to expect. Dad was out of the country for work, so I was frightened at what we would experience when the team left. This would either aggravate the spirits or give them peace. Either way, we hoped we could get some answers as to what was going on with Sharon and why so many souls were trapped here. As we were introduced to the team, they all seemed lovely people and genuine in their knowledge of the paranormal. They were totally riveted with the house and its dark past. We began our walkthrough telling them the history as we entered each room, followed by our experiences. They found it exciting, hoping they would get the same experience for one night as we do regularly. I was the least excited. I feared for Mum and Victoria when everyone left. They would be home alone after the investigation and I know this was selfish of me, but I didn't want to stay with them. I was finally away from all this and although I wanted to see what the night had in store. I didn't want to be left in fear sleeping there for the night. I knew what the 'entities' were capable of, and I didn't want to stick around when they came out. With such luck, Kate was able to come for the night. She was thrilled that a team took such interest in the house and was joyed to be invited by Mum to accompany them.

Before they even started their investigation, when taking pictures just outside the front of the house, they caught what looked to be like a tall figure behind them in the archway leading into the courtyard. You can clearly see what looks to be a head, shoulders and part of a torso. The spirit looked to be wearing some sort of hat or cap. This was the same man I saw all those years ago outside walking along the back laneway. This was clearly 'Barney'. I often think, did he know what was going on that night? Was he aware the team was there to make contact? If this was what they were already capturing at the beginning of the investigation, what was going to follow?

The team set up all their equipment throughout the house and set up a base in the large sitting room just off the reception hallway. They had cameras set up from one end of the house to the other, mainly focusing on the library, dining room, Mum and Victoria's room and the coachman's. One of the investigators walked with us filming each part of the night, hoping to capture something compelling.

As we made our way around the house Kate would pick up in each room if she felt a spirit with us. In the kitchen we all could feel a breeze sweep from one end of the room to the other. I mentioned how this would usually be the Blue Lady's walkway. This was her, possibly making her presence known to us. When moving through the rooms, we could feel the change in atmosphere. There was a sense of heaviness in the house, but it was unclear as to what it was. It could have been caused by old emotions or energies surrounding us, or maybe something more sinister lurked in the shadows curious as to what was happening. When entering the library, we sat for a moment just to gather ourselves and get a feel for our surroundings. Without any cause Mum just burst into tears. She couldn't understand why she was crying. She felt such sadness. Kate rushed to her side, and as she held her hands, she asked her to concentrate on her breathing. Kate knew exactly what was happening. Mum felt Mrs Waller's presence around her. This overwhelming feeling of emotions was from her spirit; these were her last memories of that fateful night. Unknowingly, Mum was channelling her but felt fear as she didn't feel in control of it. This was the first time she channelled a spirit and it wouldn't be her last! With the library being the room where the dark history took place, the walls absorbed an imprint of emotions from that night and everyone could feel it. Kate felt Mrs Waller's presence linger in the entranceway of the room. One of the team members began to stare towards the door; they could see a figure standing watching us from the reception hall. It didn't seem to enter but watched us from afar.

Moving into the coachman's I was apprehensive. I knew whatever was in there was waiting for me and that I would be the bait for this part of the investigation. I was familiar with most of the equipment the team used but the one that fascinated me the most was the spirit box. To hear a spirit's voice come through so clear gave me the chills. Walking closer towards the coachman's I could feel the oppressiveness. When entering the bedroom, it was freezing cold. Even though the heating had been on for a few hours prior, there was an eerie cold feel through the house. Especially within the coachman's!

We entered the bedroom and sat in a circle. As the lead investigator called out to the spirits, a few of us started to feel a presence come around. It felt like something had just entered the room. This was the best time to turn on the spirit box. If this 'spirit' wanted to make contact, surely it would talk to us through this device. The spirit box wasn't on a few seconds when a voice came through. Mum and I just looked at each other in total astonishment. When asked what was the name of the spirit that resides in the coachman's it gave the name Geoff! Okay, so this was obviously the name of the 'tall figure' I kept seeing while living in the coachman's. I couldn't help but think, if he was a human spirit why did he make me feel so ill? Why was he trying to hurt me? It didn't add up. Could it be masking itself behind this so-called 'Geoff'? Whatever was in there was sinister, it was pure evil, and its intentions were bad.

The name 'Geoff' repeated over and over again through the spirit box. The team were fascinated that the same name continued to come through the device. It was validation that whatever was in 'here' was in fact making contact and it was intelligent. Of course, it wasn't long before what I dreaded the most. "EMMA!!" My name began to repeat over and over again through the device. When asked what it wanted with Emma, it just kept repeating, "Emma, Emma, Emma." ...And again this was an intelligent answer.

This so-called spirit was trying to get to me. It knew my fear for it grew stronger and once I heard my name, it gained from that. It seemed to feed off female energy more so. When asked if he liked women he answered over the device, "I love 'em." This didn't make sense to us now, but further down the line it would. When sitting in the darkness hearing this device talk, it made everything we'd been through feel more real. This was no trick of the mind or our imagination, this was evidence of the paranormal.

Moving on to the cellar, it was another part of the investigation that I dreaded. I would never venture alone into the cellar. I feel that whatever exists in there is extremely strong and very negative. I've felt it since the first day I moved into the house. As soon as I walk close to the cellar door, I feel instantly on edge. Like something could pounce through the door and drag you in. Even today, going into the cellar I need someone with me. I don't trust what is in there. I felt I needed to show a brave face and go down with the team. Just to see what lurked down there. Maybe I could get answers as to what it was.

The team set up further pieces of equipment and explained to me and Mum how each one worked. It was all so captivating seeing these devices in action. It was the first time anything like this had ever been used in the house, so it was new to us as well as the spirits. It's possible the curiosity of the spirits made the devices work best. As we began the vigil, we could hear noises come from the far end of the cellar, right beside the staircase. It was hard to describe what we heard. Noises seemed to come from within the walls. It sounded like scratching and tapping from the other side. This was impossible. It couldn't be an animal or bird because we were underground. The lead investigator called out, "Is the spirit that's making these noises of the girl who is buried behind the wall?" Again there was tapping coming from what sounded to be behind the wall. Was this of the young girl? Or maybe something more sinister that was lurking in there, inviting it to communicate. We agreed it was time to move on.

Early morning was near, but the team felt they had unfinished business in the coachman's. When entering the room again, some of the team felt the same feeling I would have when living here. It felt as though you couldn't breathe, like someone had cut off the air supply. The energy was heavy, consuming each corner of the room. This was a different feeling from before! Because the team wanted to document the investigation, each room had cameras set up, hoping to catch the evidence that could change people's perspective on the paranormal. But the camera in the coachman's had been switched off which was recording just moments before we left for the cellar. The team were puzzled. It wasn't any of us because we were all accounted for and no one else was in the house. They noticed that the camera was not turning on. They checked batteries and wires going to and from the monitor, but all were working perfectly. The camera was then swapped from the coachman's to another room where it worked completely fine. They brought the working camera to the coachman's to try again, but it wouldn't work. This had never happened to the team before. They were taken aback as to what was wrong. Everything they had done to make the cameras work, failed! I knew then that the 'entity' that was there did not want to be seen. This was something way more intelligent than we first thought. The male spirit, supposedly 'Geoff' who hours before was able to communicate through the spirit box, now was affecting the cameras.

From the moment the cameras stopped working, each battery-operated device that was brought into the coachman's was drained almost immediately. It was near the witching hour, allegedly the strongest time for the paranormal to walk the earth's plane. I think this 'thing' was draining all its energy from these devices to do something to scare us. It was okay for the team. They were able to leave Sharon, while Mum and Victoria would be mounted with the after-effects. I was nervous for what 'it' was capable of. As the investigation came to a close, the team was left stunned by their experiences. In their eyes, Sharon

Rectory was one spiritually active location. It was a property they wouldn't forget.

The next day, I came home to talk to Mum about the investigation. When entering the house, the heaviness was still there. It was as though the energy was charged through the whole place. Mum and Victoria had a restless night from the hours that remained. They told me they heard the sounds of dragging furniture downstairs, like someone was rearranging the room. This would continue for hours. Both were scared to investigate as they lay there wishing for morning. We were physically and mentally drained the following day. I felt just like I did the years I lived in the coachman's, exhausted, sick and depressed. Just when I thought I had shaken the feeling. I relived it again. I knew my gut feeling was right about the negativity that bounded Sharon and last night confirmed it. Seeing the footage of the investigation that was sent to us by the team, proved that what was going on in the house was most certainly paranormal. From the mysterious knocks and bangs, to the bright flashing orbs and strange disembodied voices, we were amazed at how many unexplainable things they caught. But for us the most astonishing thing was the picture evidence of a spirit walking through the archway into the courtyard. It was no wonder the team were keen to get back for another investigation. Now that the first paranormal team had come and seen first-hand what happens in Sharon Rectory, it was only going to be time before more paranormal seekers wanted to see how active the house is for themselves.

Chapter XIII

Acouple of weeks passed after the investigation, and Dad continued to travel for work. I think that because we had solid evidence that something paranormal was going on, it lay in the back of my parents' mind. We've always known the house was haunted but to have a professional team conduct an investigation with equipment they claimed gathered paranormal evidence, it made it all more real. When the activity escalated, Mum and Victoria would dread going to bed at night. Victoria would often stay in Mum's room for company when Dad was away. There was feeling of relief when Dad came home from his travels. At least Mum and Victoria would sleep sounder at night. Maybe because he showed no fear, it would back down. Things seemed to settle once he was home. They still heard the usual strange noises, but nothing as sinister as what they were experiencing. While he was home it remained calm. But this would be the calm before the storm.

Mum continued to have strange dreams each night. One of which happened a couple of days before Halloween of 2013. She explains, "I drifted into a deep sleep. I had dreamt that two of the psychic mediums from the development circle were walking through the house with me. When I entered my bedroom, both mediums stopped behind in Victoria's room. As I turned to wait, I saw a young woman standing at the opposite end of the bedroom. She didn't speak but she grabbed my attention. I couldn't see her face. It seemed that there was a mist around her that hazed over her face. I turned to call for my acquaintances in the other room, but I couldn't speak. I tried shouting to them again, but nothing! I could feel myself starting to panic. The lady turned her back to me and started to walk. She slowly moved through the room and went straight into the mirror that was attached to the wardrobe. As she disappeared, I turned. Suddenly I was in another house. Terrified, I began to look around trying to find a way out. There were so many rooms but no windows, just corridors and opened doors. I was stuck in a dark hallway looking in each room for a way out.

"I came upon a room which had a small basket in the corner. I didn't know where it came from. As I walked closer to the basket, I was curious as to what was in it. I could hear something shuffling and when I looked in, I saw a small baby. I felt immediate evil from it. Like it was a spawn of the devil. I remember repeating, 'You're evil, pure evil!" to the baby. I tried running, but the corridor seemed to go on forever. I ended up in another dark room. My uncle who had passed away a few years previous appeared in front of me. Behind him was a man with a pale white face. Again, the presence of evil was strong, not from my uncle but from 'what' was behind him. I say 'what' because it was only a fragment of a human. I started to shout, 'YOU ARE EVIL... EVIL... EVIL... EVIL...' I abruptly woke from the nightmare screaming, 'EVIL,' in slow motion."

This man seemed to represent EVIL and was now entering dreams. Did he pose as a young woman and a baby to lure Mum in? Only Mum could sense the evil through her intuition. Her uncle was possibility sending a message of warning. What we needed to know was, what was this white-faced man's intention? A couple of days after, she woke again around 7.30am with a man shouting in her bedroom, "HEY!" like he was becoming inpatient. This wicked entity was getting frustrated. He was clearly trying to get to Mum, but she wasn't letting him succeed.

A couple of weeks passed; a few people from the psychic circle got together for our usual traditional meeting at Sharon. Mum told them about the strange dreams she was having. What this pale-faced man seemed to represent and how his disembodied voice would wake her on the regular basis. They suggested a walk around just to see if they could pick up this malevolent spirit. I think a few already knew where the source of this lay. Upstairs felt different. Mum's bedroom always felt warm and safe even during the darker times, but this felt as though something disrupted that aura. It was no wonder Mum was finding it difficult to sleep. A few of the group were being pulled to the coachman's. This energy seemed to leak from here. It was as if whatever was restricted to the coachman's was now given free rein to walk the full upper level of the house. Again, when crossing the threshold of the arch bedroom I felt instantly insecure. I knew this was the same 'thing' that had been terrorising me. Now it was starting to terrorise Mum. One of the ladies from the group started to pick up on a strong male energy. She could hear him mock us as we tried to figure out what he wanted. He didn't belong to the house. He didn't die here. He came from somewhere else and now claimed the coachman's as his own. She explained how 'he' used to watch me during my time living there. That he knew I felt uncomfortable with his presence. He grew attached, but it was only ever ominous. He liked to terrorise for his own thrill.

One of the other ladies walked into the bathroom

and stood close to the wall beside the shower. She could feel a strong pull of energy coming from this point. It was as if there was a gateway from another dimension. She could feel souls pass through here. It was all starting to become clear. Just directly opposite this part of the house lays an old well. There is a theory that running water can power paranormal activity. Could this water on the property have the potential for these unexplainable happenings and manifestations? Spirits can draw their energy from electromagnetic fields and running water does this.

It was known to us by word of mouth, as Sharon Rectory laid abandoned, groups of people would break in and use Ouija boards on the property. We believe now that this could be a link to this spiritual gateway in Sharon. The water from the well continues to fuel the energy for the unwanted spirits in the house. I also wondered if it was possible that the brutal assassinations from the beginning fuelled this source. I felt for once, the story behind the haunting was beginning to add up. Pieces of the puzzle were coming together. We needed to figure out how to close this spiritual portal, but it proved to be difficult. After several attempts by various people, all failed. The only other option we had was to close the coachman's and banish whatever remained to only there. With guidance from our friends, we did just that. This was only going to put a band aid over the problem, but it was a start until we sought further advice from someone who could close this portal and rid the house of these spirits.

Late November Mum woke around 5am to the smoke alarm going off in the hallway outside her bedroom door. In shock, she jumped up in the bed and listened for a moment. The alarm seemed to go off then stop for a moment before going off again. She gathered herself before opening the door. She dreaded to open it in case it was possibly a fire, and of course all she thought was, *It would be typical now when Vincent's away.* When she opened the door, the alarm suddenly turned off. She hesitated before walking downstairs to make sure everything was okay. Checking if everything was switched off and safe, Mum shook her head and thought, *It's probably the batteries going in the alarm.*

Meanwhile Victoria was still in bed alone. She too was awakened by the alarm and was a bit freaked in case something was wrong. She sat up in the bed waiting for Mum's return when she heard a man whisper in her ear, "You got big at school." Victoria looked around but saw nothing; she lay down and put the covers over her head, waiting patiently for Mum to come back. As Mum got back to bed, soon as she lay down, she heard a man's voice say, "Hello." It seemed to have come from nowhere. Victoria heard it too.

"Mum, someone whispered in my ear when you

were downstairs." Victoria continued to tell her. Struggling to fall back asleep again, they remained awake for the remaining hours. Who was this man that was making himself known? Could it be Mr Waller or maybe another acquaintance? They would try not to let it affect them. They chose to ignore further activity even though it terrified them. Being alone when it happened made things harder. Victoria continued to stay in Mum's room while Dad was away. They would stay up and watch TV until they fell asleep, just so there was a noise, other than pure silence.

Only a few nights after hearing the voice, they woke to three loud bangs coming somewhere within the bedroom. Mum turned to Victoria and reassured her, telling her to ignore them. She put on a brave front for her; knowing that Mum was scared too, it would only make things worse for Victoria. But whatever malevolent spirit it was, continued to bang in all corners of the room. It clearly knew it was being ignored and wasn't happy about it. Mum explained how the feeling in the room changed that night. It felt more sinister and wanted them to be scared. They couldn't wait for Dad to be home; they started to count the days to his return. Knowing this was happening, I suggested for them to come stay with me. But Mum stood her ground. "It will not scare me from my home." And right she was. I didn't want her feeling scared in her own home. She knew she had to stand up to it. But I didn't want them being on their own, so I told them I would come stay. It was the right thing to do. They were terrified and even though I was scared too, I wanted to be there for them. Gabriel too was away for work, so it made sense for us to stay together.

I took the travel cot with me and Noah and I stayed in Victoria's room. It had been years since I stayed in there and it felt weird. As I lay in the bed the memories rushed back. There I was, back in 1997, a scared little child again. The bed was in the exact same place where I would lay at night and look at the window above the door. Whatever it was about the window, I hated it. Maybe knowing the coachman's was just a couple of rooms away made me nervous. That and the fact the dreaded back staircase was just at the other side of the door. I kept the door through to my parents room opened and put Noah's cot beside the bed nearest to the door of Mum's room. I could see straight through from where I lay in the bed. At least if either of them would wake with anything strange, I would too be able to see. I kept the beside light on and struggled to fall sleep. Every few minutes I would roll over to check on Noah. A part of me worried for him being here, but I had no other choice. I drifted in and out of sleep most of the night. I gave in and stayed awake for the last few hours. I just dreaded staying there, I was so restless.

As I turned and lay there watching into my parents' room, I started to feel pure heaviness come over my body. I couldn't move my legs, arms or turn my head. I was completely frozen in the bed. I tried to scream for Mum, but no words would come out. I started to break into a cold sweat. I could sense something in the room with me, but I couldn't move to see. All I could think of was Noah. He lay there fast asleep. I could see him from where I lay. It took all my strength to break free from whatever hold came over me. What felt like hours, was probably only minutes. I sat up in the bed to look around, but nothing was there. It was the most intense attack I'd had. I was petrified. Whatever was causing this really did feed off fear and it was becoming dangerous. I told Mum once they woke what happened. I knew I couldn't stay another night. Not knowing what could happen next, I didn't want to risk it with Noah in the house.

On Dads return from work, roughly a week later, both him and Mum were home alone this evening. When sitting in the kitchen, it is very hard to hear if someone is at the front entrance, but sometimes our little dog would let us know by barking outside the window. Late that night, our dog started to bark uncontrollably. Dad looked out of the kitchen window to check what had caught the dog's attention. It ran around to the front entrance, which indicated that she had caught a glimpse of something. Dad went to the front porch and opened the door. No-one was there. He walked out to the street and around the far end of the house. Our dog continued to bark at something towards the front porch. All of a sudden, he heard a loud bang off one of the windows to the library. It shook with the vibration.

Dad was directly outside at this point and when he looked around, again no-one was there. He thought, *Maybe it was a bat hitting the window,* but when checking, nothing was there. He described the sound as if something had hit the window with force. In the meantime, the dog continued to bark. She looked at Dad, then back in the direction of the house. It was as if the dog was trying to warn him of something. He found it strange but couldn't find an explanation. This knocking continued on and off for weeks after; it mainly occurred at night when everyone was in bed. The sound would echo throughout the house, so it was hard to distinguish exactly where it came from. I believe it was the unhinged spirit that seemed to lurk in the shadows, watching as they slept.

Voices seemed to come from nowhere and Mum quite often heard this disembodied voice. At times it would sound very deep, with a growl-like reverberation, then other times soft like a young child. This seemed to either mimic spirits or had multiple personalities, but either way we didn't know what it was.

Chapter XIV

The beginning of 2014 I found out I was
pregnant with my second child. We were over
the moon that Noah would grow up with a
companion. I know this will sound strange, but I felt I
needed to avoid visiting the house while pregnant.
With how I felt in my last pregnancy I wanted to stay
away when possible. Whenever Dad was home from
his travels, Victoria would sometimes stay at mine just
to get a full night's sleep. She too was struggling being
in the house at night. She often saw and heard things
that would become more malicious as time went on. I
suggested for her to stay at mine when Dad was home
with Mum. The fear that grew with me, I didn't want
for her or my own children. I wanted to protect them
for as long as I could from the evil that lurked over
Sharon. Although the house looked its best, the
feeling just didn't match to how it beheld.

Every March the house would often release a surge

of energy. We always put it down to it being the anniversary of Reverend Hamilton and Mrs Waller's murder. It was as though it was a ripple effect passing down through the centuries. I wouldn't say it is the most active time of the year. It feels like a different dynamic. A sadness, as such. We grew to understand the terms behind what type of haunting we were dealing with. We knew this was the residual energy remaining from the 2nd of March. From this date and for weeks after we would experience various occurrences that tend to happen during this time. There always seems to be a darkness that lingers around the house, especially then. On the weeks approaching the anniversary of 2014, Mum often woke again with the smoke alarm going off during the night. When checking the house, there never seemed to be a reason why it would trigger or turn on. It only ever was the smoke alarm outside Mum's bedroom in the hallway, which she found strange. After changing batteries and checking it numerous times, they could never determine what the cause was.

On the evening of the 7th of March, while Mum and Dad sat in the kitchen, they heard our dog bark outside. She always alerted us when a car was approaching or if someone was outside and because Victoria had her friend up, Mum thought it was her parents coming to lift her. When Dad looked out, he didn't see or hear a car. Not thinking too much of it, they carried on watching TV. After a few minutes, the dog continued to bark vigorously outside. Confused and wondering what was wrong with the dog, Dad walked up the hall to the front porch to check again. He opened the door and called out to the dog. She looked to be drawn to the roof above the library. He walked out and looked up. He could see bright sparks coming from under the roof tiles. After a few seconds he realised the roof was on fire. In an instant, he ran down to Mum to call for the fire brigade. Mum stood in shock. She reached for the phone and rang me. I answered and she continued to tell me that the house was on fire. After calming her I asked her if she rang the fire brigade. She panicked and said, "Hold on until I check if it is on fire." She was in total denial. I came off the phone and drove straight to Sharon.

After Mum contacted the emergency services, she ran up to Dad in the reception room hallway. He was trying to salvage what furniture and anything he could grab. I pulled up outside and saw that the fire had started to creep through the roof fascia. I tried to get my parents, Victoria and her friend out of the house. We stood and watched the blaze grow as the fire brigade approached. The firefighters got straight to work. Not realising how big the blaze would be, they only had a certain amount of water accessible when they landed. More crews were called from close by stations. Soon enough, the street was crammed with emergency service vehicles. They all needed to access the back laneway because the narrow front drive wouldn't let them reach the property. As some of the firefighters went to find local water points to refill their tanks, it proved difficult. My Uncle Raymond soon surveyed and with his good thinking they remembered about the well at the rear of the house. Quickly, they went with a generator through the overgrown grass trying to find the manhole cover which enclosed the well.

Everyone seemed to panic because the fire began to burn through the building. Dad couldn't sit back and watch for much longer. He grabbed one of the water pipes from the men and charged through the front door, risking his life to stop the blaze. The adrenalin pumped through his veins giving him the strength to continue on. To my parents, their whole life was going up in flames before their very eyes. Dad saw how distraught Mum was and his first reaction was to fight it. I tried to console Mum. We knew it was going to be difficult coming back from this.

After what felt like hours, was probably only minutes, Dad reappeared. We tried to get him over to the ambulance to be checked over, but he refused. While we stood outside, we could see the fire burning red through the windows of the library. Pieces of the ceiling were falling, ripping everything from the walls that surrounded it. The fire creeped into the reception hallway towards the cellar doorway. The fire chief approached Mum and I, reassuring us that they were doing all they could to save our home. We were trying to come to terms with the worst. After we encouraged Dad to be checked by the paramedics, they advised him to be taken to hospital because of smoke inhalation. But I knew they had other concerns. Mum refused to leave the house. I believed that a part of her died that night in the fire. She was so disheartened from the years she put into making this house her home. I know what she lost was just 'things', but to her they were much more.

The hours seemed to fly by. It was the early hours of the morning before the fire was contained. The fire crew worked their hardest through the night. The once beautiful room with original shuttering and structure was no more. It lay as the shell it once was. As the firefighters began to pack away the remaining tools and equipment, one of the men approached myself and Mum. He asked if either of us had entered the house during the time of the fire. We looked at each other and shook our heads with a NO! He said, "Myself and a few of the men saw a woman standing in the hallway near the large staircase. She seemed to watch as the fire burned through the reception room hallway." We were in shock. There was no other woman there, only me and Mum.

She looked at me and said, "That was her, wasn't

it?"

The firefighter seemed to freeze on the spot. He said, "I don't even want to know!" They weren't familiar with the stories or our experiences over the years, but our reactions to his question spooked him. I left for the hospital once the crew were finished. Our neighbour came up and stayed with Mum while I went to visit Dad. He was worse off than I thought. He seemed confused and very drowsy. After speaking with the doctor, he told me Dad had a heart attack during the fire. Because there was such a release of adrenaline through his body, he was unable to feel the attack occur. It was just as well that Dad wasn't there to see the results of the blaze. Seeing the house in its final state would have killed him. I worried for both my parents, and in my current state I didn't want the stress to get to me.

I tried to get Mum to leave Sharon and come home with me, but she was determined that she would not be leaving the house. I could only support her decision. I knew I couldn't add to her anxiety. We brought what we could retrieve from the main building into the coachman's, but with smoke and water damage only some things were salvageable. With the coachman's at the opposite end of the house, it was the only part which wasn't damaged and still was liveable. We were lucky in a sense that no-one was asleep when the fire broke out. If it wasn't for our trusty little hound warning everyone of the danger, they would only have noticed when it was too late. I tried to reassure Mum that things would be fixed over time. She needed to focus on getting Dad back to better health and to worry about the restoration later.

The following few days were just as hard. The press soon got wind of the blaze and began to print false stories to sell papers. I took it upon myself to contact each one, reminding them of our privacy and their false accusations of how the fire started. It continued for days with the media and noisy bystanders coming onto the property to view what was left. It got to the point where we needed 24-hour surveillance because Mum started to feel unsafe. Close friends helped board up windows which were blown out during the blaze. At least this made entering the house difficult for anyone who tried breaking in.

It was cramped in the coachman's for Mum and Victoria only because they had so much stuff that they tried to store in there while everyone got to work clearing the rubble from the main house. Dad was still in hospital and awaited further treatment in Galway so he could make a full recovery. For me, this was probably the most stressful time for us. Even after the previous years of sleepless nights and fear of the unknown, it wasn't anything in comparison to this. I felt helpless!

Because I was only in my first trimester of pregnancy, not many people knew. I felt people would only assume that I would be the person to set up and help Mum while Dad was recovering. But she remained strong and determined to do as much as she could herself. During their stay in the coachman's, like clockwork both Mum and Victoria would hear the gates of the archway to the courtyard bang against the wall every night around 10:30. The first time it happened they froze still on the sofa. Knowing that it was only them in the house they worried it might have been trespassers roaming the grounds, mistaken that the house was still occupied. Mum stood at the door and put on the outside light which shone throughout the bottom of the courtyard. This would at least warn intruders that someone was in the house. They looked outside but saw no-one and the gates remained opened. They didn't seem to hear anything else that night. But the same sound repeated the following night and so on. This occurred nightly during their stay in the coachman's. It was so strange to me. This had never happened while I lived there. This makes me think that maybe the spirit of 'Barney' who wanders the grounds, felt obligated to close the entrance gates to the courtyard to protect prowlers from entering? Even though these were phantom sounds from the gates, to him this was his way of protecting the house. I know that the spirits who reside in Sharon Rectory are intelligent and they respond to all that happens with the house. I believe that Mrs Waller knew her home that she loved so dear, was in danger of burning to the ground that awful night. It had to have been her that stood and watched among the burning flames. And as for Barney, it was his duty as caretaker and groundsman to close the gates surrounding Sharon to ensure its security from intruders onto the property.

During their stay in the coachman's, Mum struggled to sleep every night. She didn't feel right somehow. It felt very uncomfortable for her. Maybe because she wasn't used to sleeping in another room in the house or maybe it was 'something' that was in there that made her feel this insecure. She couldn't wait until morning, when night fell, and she had to go to sleep. Keeping focused on the rebuild took her mind off the feelings in the coachman's. She too felt the same uneasiness as I did when I first moved in. She would wake in cold sweats with feelings of being watched. Victoria also feared for what was in there.

Weeks had passed and the forensics came back with the conclusion that a wire in the attic from the large chandelier in the reception room hallway had been burning for days before the fire broke out. Mice had nibbled at the wire causing a break in the cable, enabling a spark and the surrounded dust to ignite. This was unknown to us. They advised in future to place a smoke alarm in all attic spaces to ensure no further fires. This was something you never would think to happen, but it gave us peace of mind that it wasn't something sinister. The restoration took months before it became liveable, and now that Dad had made a full recovery and was in better health, he wanted to get stuck in and make Sharon Rectory as beautiful as it once was before. His plan was to rebuild the third level that once existed many moons ago. He wanted to bring the original look back to the patio side of the house. This would have once been the main rooms within the house, where Mr and Mrs Waller lived, while the first and second storey were for the master and his servants. Dad wanted to look at this as a new project. It would be the next chapter in Sharon's history as such. He had a very precise vision. It was as if something was guiding him in the renovation. Also, Mum seemed to have a different approach with the decorating; she and Dad were changing the look of the home that I once knew. But it seemed to work. They were doing everything right. Certain rooms were now decorated how I'd have pictured it over a hundred years ago but with a modern twist. They would still have a long way to go but it was a start to a new and exciting change to Sharon Rectory.

After a few hectic months, Mum got in touch with our friends from the psychic development class. We planned to regroup in Sharon for the first time after the fire. The rooms in the main house were almost complete and everyone was excited to see the on-going renovations. They wanted to have a walk through to see how the energies felt after such tragedy and knowing there would be a disruption to the spirits after the fire and renovations, it was going to be interesting. They were curious to see what they would pick up. One girl who was new to the psychic group, was great at capturing strange and unexplainable things in photos. She had caught some really extraordinary things in the past which makes me think that spirits seem to be drawn to her. We were excited to see what she would catch during this visit.

She began to snap some pictures and as we entered the coachman's the same horrible feeling remained. It would catch you as you crossed the threshold into the arch bedroom. She continued to take photos automatically, without focusing anywhere in particular. When walking down the stairs of the coachman's it was ice cold. You could almost see your breath when we spoke, and the musty smell lingered in the room even after it had been decorated. Mum told us that during her stay in there, the kitchen/living space would never heat, even with the log fire burning. This was also the case when I lived there. We could never explain how one place could be so cold. It isn't the kind of temperature one would expect when the heating is off, but a chill that hits you to your core. Without us realising, something compelling was caught in one of the photos that was taken in that moment. We didn't realise until our friend went through all the pictures afterwards. In this picture, you can clearly see a reflection of a bald man with no apparent features. Beside him is a reflection of a woman who also has no facial features. What makes it even more frightening, there were NO men with us that night. So, we can't rule him out as one of the group. This was so disturbing to us. Could this be the 'tall shadow man' that haunted me during my time in the coachman's as well as making Mum and Victoria uncomfortable? We now had the actual proof of this unkindly chap, but who was this woman that shadowed this malevolent one and why wasn't she present before now?

Chapter XV

After another long and eventful year, our little family was complete with the arrival of my second son Jonah. The boys brought so much joy to what seemed to be the darkest of years upon us. It had been a rough time with the stresses of a rebuild, but Mum was finally getting her home back. With so much work still left to do, the lower level of the house was now finished. Of course, there were things that were lost that could never been replaced, but as long as our family was safe, nothing else mattered. The main house did feel slightly lighter, especially in the library. Mum has a theory that this room, which holds such sadness and despair, needed to be cleansed of its horrid memories that saw a beautiful woman lose her life over the quarrel of a distant friend and his enemies. We had hoped this to be a new start, and an end to the suffering of many spirits that laid uneasy within the house.

Victoria's senses were developing more the older she got. She wasn't encouraged or asked to talk about what she saw or felt but approached us daily with things that we couldn't see. There were some that scared her, but also good that she knew she shouldn't fear. It wasn't only in Sharon where she saw these spirits, but places she would visit. She would often say to Mum about the 'shadow people' she would see in hospitals or isolated roads when passing. Not knowing about a place's history, she could tell if there was a tragedy by seeing these lost souls wandering, looking for help. There was a period where she struggled with closing herself off from the spirit world. Now in her mid-teens, this was the time she needed to learn how to flip that switch off, so she could concentrate on her studies. She was bullied in school for being different and for living in a house that people would often joke about, giving its history with hauntings. We tried to not let this damage her. It was similar to when I grew up, but with today's youths having access to mobile phones and social media, there was no escape from these cowards that taunted her. We needed her to focus on rising up from the darkness and be proud of being unique.

Given that sometimes there was no escape from the living as well as the dead, she fell into a dark depression. The pattern of despair and hopelessness fell among us all during our years in Sharon and when entering into this state, it's hard to see a way out. With the added pressure from her peers, Victoria refused to go to school. She lay in her darkened bedroom until midday, wallowing. We were overcome with worry. She was so young to have these feelings and live with such guilt from being different. Mum had many sleepless nights as Victoria would get up in the middle of the night to run away. But I felt there was more to it. There was more at play here. I too had been down this road when I was in my late teens. Could this be an attachment from this entity that resided in Sharon? And maybe it too fed off her depression. With the on-going renovations to Sharon, I felt something may have been disrupted again along the way. While the main house felt quiet and more peaceful, the eastern side to the house had a heaviness to it. To me, it felt like it started from Victoria's room straight through to the coachman's residence. I wanted to sit Victoria down and find out what she was thinking. I needed to get into her head because I too could relate to this feeling. When questioning her on why she felt the need to run away, she seemed to struggle with explaining it. She wasn't a person for sleepwalking, nor would she be spontaneous enough to go outside in the dark on her own, and I knew this. She felt like she didn't know what overcame her in that moment. It was like something made her do it! I wasn't sure what to think. This could have been an ominous source at work here, or maybe it was her subconscious saving her from whatever was spiritually attacking her while she was feeling down. I told Mum I had concerns that the same entity that once caused my breakdown years previous, could also be what Victoria was experiencing. We knew this 'thing' from the coachman's was bound to that area before the fire, but when Mum, Dad and Victoria stayed there, this obviously broke that binding. As Victoria was the most vulnerable out of the three, she was the perfect energy source for it. Before, this entity had been blocked from having the run of the house; living in the same environment gave it the time to work on Victoria. This would explain why the eerie feel that was once allocated to the coachman's was now in Victoria's bedroom.

When Gabriel got a new job in November 2015, it required him to work away from home quite a bit. I started to struggle with the boys, being on my own, and I needed to be closer to Mum, but finding other accommodation was difficult. I made the decision to move home. Even though it seemed like a bad idea to put myself and my children back into that environment, I felt that something was drawing me home to the rectory. Maybe this on-going issue with Victoria made me want to be there and show support to both her and my parents. But in the other hand, I didn't want to be back in the negative atmosphere of the coachman's knowing that different energies were resurfacing. We had tried and tested the different approaches to clearing what was in there, but we knew we needed that certain someone with the ability to finally rid our home of this entity. Anyone who we thought could help, failed. It would only ever give a few weeks of peace before stirring up again. So, before I moved back, I prepped myself mentally for this change. My sons on the other hand, how could I tell two small children that we were moving into a scary place but not to fear it? I couldn't! It was up to me to protect them and I was going to do all I could to do that. It was going to be different this time; I felt stronger mentally and spiritually but physically I still would struggle.

Only recently being diagnosed with fibromyalgia, I was learning how to cope with the physical pain as well as trying different things to benefit me so I could be at my healthiest. Stress was one of the triggers, so I knew the move with two small children would be stressful enough without having to worry about the 'extras' that came with the coachman's. While we moved some of the old furniture out into storage, I decided to burn sage and do my own blessings in the flat. Even though this had been done many times before by various different people, I thought maybe it would have more of an effect from me because I once lived in the coachman's and was gracing it once again. I needed to stand my ground to all unworldly entities within it. As I started to move my things back home, the heaviness didn't feel as intense.

The arch bedroom was right next door; this was where the boys would sleep. I thought the first couple of weeks would be the hardest granted the boys were in a new environment. I had a lot of sleepless nights in the beginning, but with our energies and the constant busyness of two young children, it didn't feel as bad as it once did. Hoping that things were finally settling, it wasn't long before it was back to how it once felt. I often burned sage and cleared the flat, but this would only help for a few days before the heaviness took hold once again. I hadn't yet seen 'the tall man' that scared me years before and I dreaded for that time to come, because I knew it would. I knew it was still there. I could sense him. And that picture which we captured of the spirit man and woman, always plagued in the back of my mind. I was so glad on the days Gabriel came home. I tried not to show fear. I knew this was what 'it' fed on, but sometimes the terror just took over.

It wasn't long before I felt that 'something' was spooking the boys. They often slept in the bed next to me which gave that sense of security, knowing they were within arm's reach. But in the arch bedroom, they would never settle. I did feel nervous with them being in there on their own. I prayed every night for these spirits and entities to just leave us alone. I wouldn't say I'm religious, but I needed some faith to help battle this. I knew something had to be done. Even though 'they' too refused to leave, I was determined to make them.

We got in touch with Kate again. She was the only person we felt we could turn to during these times. I had hoped that she could give us the advice we needed. We arranged for her visit; I thought I would do my own bit of investigating. I wanted to see if I could catch anything unusual on video while we slept. At least this would be more proof that something had been taunting us while we slept. Darkness fell and after getting the boys down for the night, I set up the camera on my phone to record. I didn't have any fancy equipment or camcorders, so this was the next best thing. The chances of me getting anything in 40 minutes were slim, but it was worth a try. I don't know how I managed it, but I fell asleep pretty quickly that night. I always kept the bathroom light on which shone through into the bedroom. I could never sleep in total darkness. It is a completely different atmosphere when in total darkness.

I woke in the morning and reviewed the video. I was shocked at what I saw. Just 15 minutes into the video you can hear phantom footsteps walk down the stairs from the arch bedroom and into the coachman's. A few seconds after, the light to the bathroom switches off and the bedroom turns into complete darkness. For the rest of the video the room stays in darkness, but the sounds of the footsteps continue. I was in shock! When I woke, the bathroom light was still on. I couldn't explain it. I checked if the other electrics had been turned off to rule out a power surge, but nothing. Only the bathroom light had been turned off. I doubted myself for many years whether I had seen something turn the light on and off, but never had the proof to say otherwise.

It was a few days after, we had the visit from Kate. I had hoped she could pick up what this spirit's intentions were. I had this strange feeling and worry over my children. As much as I wanted to protect my kids from all harm, how could I protect them from something I couldn't see? I wanted more answers. On the evening of Kate's arrival, I told her what had been happening since we moved back. Her feelings had changed since the last visit. There was something new, but she couldn't figure out what it was. As we walked up the back staircase and into the arch bedroom, she felt the presence of a lady. She had never felt this lady before. It was as if she was cloaked, hidden until now. This was possibly the lady in the picture beside the 'bald man'.

As the evening's sky drew darker the atmosphere changed. We stood in the room; it felt like we were intruding into someone else's space. Kate's visions were of a lady wearing a long dress, with wispy hair gathered around her face. She felt as though she was from the wiccan community. It was unclear at this point what her intensions were. Kate could see this lady bending over Jonah's cot as though she was hushing him while he woke. This would explain why Jonah never settled in the arch-room. He obviously was scared seeing this strange lady as he woke. I had real concerns; it wasn't only the negative entity and aggressive male presence that resided in the coachman's but a wiccan who claimed the arch bedroom. I wanted to dig and find out who this male and female once were. I had hoped that if we recognised and acknowledged these spirits it may give them peace to move on. But things would only begin to make sense as time went on.

As weeks passed, we still worried for Victoria. We had got advice from friends and professionals as to what we could do with Victoria's bullying situation. It was suggested that she should be taken out of school for home schooling. We all agreed that it was the best decision for her. Other school options weren't the solution; many more bullies unearthed from surrounding areas that targeted her on social media. This ruled out a transfer. In the meantime, Victoria started to really fear going to bed at night. Something different was felt that wasn't around before now. When she told us about her first experience seeing this ghost, it surely sent shivers down my spine. While she had felt an uneasiness in her bedroom since moving back in after the fire, it took time before something apparent began to show itself to her. When walking up the back staircase she could see a rugged man in what looked to be a long white hospital gown, crawl on all fours up the staircase behind her. She screamed and ran into her bedroom closing the door behind her. She had never seen anything more frightening and her description of him was unlike anything we had seen before. This would only be the start of the torment that followed with this male presence.

Chapter XVI

As there was on-going activity straight through to Christmas, we couldn't believe how bad the house had got. And the new year wasn't going to be any better. I was beginning to give up all hope that the house would ever be rid of ghosts. Nineteen years had passed, and although there were times where we actually thought it was over, something would happen to prove otherwise. I was struggling to live in the coachman's yet again. No matter what I did, I couldn't get the boys settled. I could feel myself coming under an oppression again. Even though I tried not let it take control, the sleepless nights made it harder. More spirits came forth and we weren't sure how or why we hadn't seen or felt them before now. It seemed that once one made itself known another would appear days later. We felt like we were hitting a brick wall, nothing made sense anymore.

Mid-January of 2016, late on Monday night, Mum awoke and felt the urge to go downstairs. As she walked over by the sink, she turned and noticed a young man standing in the middle of the kitchen staring at her. She was convinced someone had broken into the house. She shouted, "What do you want?" but there was no reply. He just smiled and continued to stare at her. He wore a shirt under a jumper with a black leather jacket. She started to panic. She turned her head for a split second but when she looked back, he was gone. She checked the back door, but it remained locked. She knew it was impossible for someone to move that quickly. She was confused. If he was a spirit, he didn't look like he belonged to the house. His appearance looked fresh, like he was from then and now. He wasn't like any of the 'others' she had witnessed during her time in Sharon. It kept playing in her head. *Why would I see this person in my kitchen?* When Mum told me about this, I thought there were only two reasons this was happening. One being we had spirit attachments from God only knows where, or two, it was something to do with this 'portal' in the coachman's. This negative one from the coachman's didn't feel like he was from the house, nor did the eerie presence that Victoria saw crawl up the stairs behind her. To me, they came through this 'gateway' and claimed the residence as their own. We were thrown in the deep end from the very start. When we witnessed 'them' we needed to learn how to cope. This was only another hurdle we had to face.

A week after Mum saw this spirit man in the kitchen, Noah woke me one night telling me he saw a 'dark man' in his bedroom. I knew this was it. This had to be the tall man, 'the negative one' that I saw. He seemed very nervous in the room. I believe that all children are born with a sixth sense, but as we get older, we learn to 'tune out' from the spirit world and lose the ability to see spirits. There are only a few that continue with this 'gift'. If you wish to call it that. I wasn't ready to explain to my four-year-old son what he was seeing. I knew by my boys' reactions since we moved back that they had sensed something in the room. Jonah could not yet explain in words what he saw, but Noah knew this was a 'scary person'. Little did I know that on the same night Noah witnessed this entity, Victoria saw something equally as terrifying.

The next morning, I told Mum Noah had seen something and I knew this was the same thing I saw. Although I didn't go into detail with Noah on what he had seen, I knew already it was him. I of course comforted Noah and reassured him that it was only a bad dream. I hated lying to him, but I didn't know what else to do. I knew if Gabriel heard Noah talk about this 'man' he would think that we told him about what was going on in the house. Even though Gabriel experienced things from time to time, he didn't want to believe it was happening. He would brush it aside and pretend nothing went on. But I couldn't. I lived with it for so long. I live through the stigma, the funny looks, the stares and mumbles of the people who knew. In his eyes, he didn't sign up for this involvement with the spirits and I respected that. I would rarely talk to him about it unless I needed to. But he knew I had growing concerns when it came to the boys. Mum thought best to ask Kate's advice on this. She continued to tell me about Victoria's experience – as she got up during the night to use my parents' bathroom, she walked through the bedroom and into the wardrobe room. She noticed the airing cupboard door lay open and found it weird. When she walked closer, she could see a young girl hanging by her neck from one of the shelves. She slammed the door shut and ran back to her room. We didn't want to be contacting Kate whenever something happened, but we agreed there was a lot of energy building up in the house and these new spirits were a prime example.

Kate called to the house again. When she walked through to my parents' room, she could sense the young girl. She could pick up on the fear, either from the young girl spirit or the residue of Victoria's terror. She felt it could be the same connection to the girl who was buried in the cellar. But there was more to be discovered about this girl before she would find peace. She placed a voice recorder in the bedroom as well as the back staircase.

When entering the coachman's, she could sense two men. One of which was watching Noah. The other was the one we already knew. This other male was very unpleasant; she described him to be a farmer. He thinks this to be his home. His intentions weren't great. He had a very negative impression. He was the kind that would have done terrible things while he was alive, and he was punished greatly for it. Now, we had two hostile male spirits residing in the coachman's. This worried me! Although these males were profound the wiccan seemed to fade. Her presence wasn't as strong. It was as if the energies of the two men overpowered her. Kate knew these were reluctant to leave. It would take a lot of energy and time to rid these spirits from the coachman's. However, it was nothing that we hadn't already done before. It was just going to take time. May it be a month or another 20 years.

When Kate left that evening, she told us she would be in contact if she got anything on the voice recorders. Again, we worried about what would to come next. As we got ready for bed, I couldn't help but think, *Why did I put myself back in this situation?* Mum knew I was scared and with Gabriel working away, she suggested Victoria stay over with us in the coachman's. It wasn't like either any of us could do anything if they showed themselves, but it was someone for company. The boys remained oblivious to anything paranormal. To Noah it was only a bad dream and Jonah was too young to understand. When my parents went to bed, after a couple of hours Dad woke with knocking on the bedroom window. This was just like the first experience he had with Mrs Waller. He got up and looked out the window but of course, no one was there.

Roughly a week had passed when one evening Mum was standing in the kitchen doing her ironing. She was distracted by a very large dark shadow coming from the boiler house outside across the wall to the kitchen window where she stood. She looked out but saw no-one. A few minutes passed when she saw this large shadow again. This time it went past the window and came right up to the door. She saw the shadow clearer the second time. She knew by the looks of it, it was a man, but only saw him in the darkness. She braved it and opened the door to check but couldn't see anything. This unpleasant vibe just lingered outside, like something stood back, watching her. She got a nervous feeling in the pit of her stomach. She quickly closed the door. As she did so, the phone rang. It was Kate! It was just like she knew what had happened. She told her she had been listening to the recordings from the week before. She had caught something very compelling. She could clearly hear footsteps running up and down the back staircase. She knew where everyone was during the time of the recording, so it was amazing she had caught it. This was chilling. It's a totally different feeling when you have the solid proof of what you've been experiencing. Like I've mentioned previously, when you are experiencing it, there is that doubt in your mind whether or not it is actually happening. Even though we could set up our own cameras and equipment to detect whether or not a spirit is near. That is no way to live. We were already struggling to sleep at night without adding the extra fear.

Each week it seemed that something paranormal happened. It was the usual footsteps, shadows, doors banging, but thankfully the manifestations had stopped. The kids seemed more settled. We knew it wasn't the end, but the calmness was refreshing. It was only a matter of time before our lives would turn upside down yet again.

On the May bank holiday weekend my son Jonah sustained a concussion after a fall which led to a trip to A&E. Thankfully, he was fine with no lasting effects. On Sunday morning, Gabriel left for work. It was like any other day. I hated when he left because I knew I was alone with the kids in the coachman's. I feared we would witness this entity again. That afternoon, Jonah started to come down with a temperature following sickness. I was worried considering the fall a couple of days previous. I tried contacting Gabriel to let him know we were going back to A&E with Jonah. The phone rang until it rang out. I never read into it because I thought Gabriel was probably driving. Within the space of about 15 minutes, Gabriel rang me back. When I answered, it wasn't him. It was a paramedic. My heart dropped! I knew something bad had happened. The paramedic told me Gabriel had a been in a serious accident at work. I didn't know what to do. It was as if the world around me was in slow motion. My son was sick and now Gabriel was being transferred to a hospital miles away. I ran to my parents with the phone still in hand. If it wasn't for them, I don't know what I would have done. I didn't know Gabriel's injuries and I feared I was going to lose him. I phoned Jonah's godmother who is a very close friend and I asked for her help. Both her and Mum took Jonah to A&E, while me and Dad drove to the hospital to Gabriel.

I was relieved when Mum phoned to say Jonah was fine, but that they would keep him overnight to monitor him. Gabriel, on the other hand, wasn't. He suffered a severe break in his leg which caused the fibula and tibia to break through the skin. He underwent surgery to try save the leg. Thankfully after hours in theatre, I was able to see him. We knew he would make a full recovery. But it was an overwhelmingly stressful time. Just as I thought our lives were getting back to normal, something bad happened. I began to think was I cursed. Why was it every time I got back on track, something threw me off? I wanted to get out of the coachman's yet again. I tried finding somewhere to live that was close by. I knew that once Gabriel got out of hospital, we would need to move into a bungalow. Luckily, I found this perfect little house in the village of Newtowncunningham, just a few miles down the road. It was exactly what we needed. Soon after Gabriel got out of hospital, we moved.

A few weeks later, I finally started to feel myself getting better. But Victoria in the other hand, continued to have the oppressive feeling in her room. Her terror grew while she was in the house. To me, I believe that because she showed fear, it fuelled 'it' to become stronger. Like how my fear in the coachman's made it more apparent. On the weeks that Dad worked away, Victoria continued to stay in my parents' bedroom. Even though, regardless of who you were with, if you were going to feel or see anything paranormal, there was absolutely nothing either of you could do. This was simply for the company.

In June, Dad returned home from work. Victoria had a feeling that something was yet again building up to happen. She was experiencing footsteps running up the back staircase after her, each time she went up alone. It got to the point where Mum had to stand at the bottom of the stairs when Victoria needed to go to her bedroom. It was unclear as to what this was. I remember when I first heard the footsteps coming up the back stairs, I was so young. They were very clear and slow moving. Victoria described these as a scarpering up behind her. Like something was crawling along. This couldn't be the same thing we were experiencing.

It was late one Friday night, when Victoria had yet another unexpected visit by an inimical presence. As she lay in bed struggling to fall asleep, she could see in the corner of her eye, her wardrobe door sliding open by itself. What she saw, was extremely disturbing. She described it like a man that had escaped an insane asylum. He had a grey complexion, long straggly hair, extremely thin. He wore a long white hospital gown. She could see him rock back and forth in the corner of her wardrobe among the clothes. Victoria ran straight into my parents. She was distressed. Mum got up to investigate her wardrobe as she thought maybe Victoria might have had a bad dream. When walking into Victoria's bedroom she felt uneasiness. Victoria had begged Mum to stay in with her. But Mum is very set in her ways. She wouldn't sleep in any other room of the house, only her own bedroom. She knew Victoria was scared, so she climbed into bed and they tried to get some sleep.

After a few minutes, Mum could feel what she

describes as a creature crawl up her legs on top of the bedcovers. She couldn't move for fear. She just prayed for it to leave. Suddenly they both heard growls coming from the corner of the room beside the doorway to the back staircase. They both jumped up out of the bed and ran into Dad next door. Mum said to him to sleep in Victoria's room. Dad went next door and lay down in the bed. With Dad showing no fear, he just fell asleep. During the night, he woke with discomfort. He felt a heaviness in the room. This bedroom never used to feel as oppressive or hostile. Yes, there were times when we would see many shadows and apparitions pass through, but the heaviness was from something else. Something that claimed this space as its own. When Dad woke the next morning, he said it was one of the worst night's sleep he'd had in a long time.

Over the next week, Victoria's guard was up. When Mum told me what happened, I worried Victoria had an attachment. She was opened to seeing more things around the house, but I struggled to understand where they all came from. It seemed that every week there was something new. She needed to close herself off from it all. There was a point where she struggled to walk around the house by herself because she would see apparitions pass her in the hallways or some appeared to run after her. I had to sit her down and help her shut it off. Since Victoria had grown up in this house from birth, it was going to be difficult. This was a part of her. But if she didn't learn to control it, this would ruin her life. When you fall under attack from an oppressive spirit, it can destroy you. I feared that for Victoria. I knew what it was like to feel this lack of self-control, may it be in body or mind. And I couldn't control it, I couldn't explain it. It changes me as a person.

I sat Victoria down. She was old enough to understand that this had a possible role in her emotions. Although the bullying continued, she felt that there was more to how she was acting. The sleepless nights, the fear of seeing something else that terrified her, it all contributed to how she felt. I knew that once she could overcome one, she would be able to conquer the other. She was much stronger than me. She needed to break out of that shell to fight.

Shortly after, I saw Victoria change into a more confident young adult. She seemed to grow braver overnight. When she started to feel that fear creep over her, when she knew something unpleasant was there, she told it to f*ck off. She demanded it to leave. This was her home. Not theirs! She worked hard at blocking them out. She was learning how to control closing herself off to the spirits when she wanted to. This is difficult for any mature medium to do, never mind someone of Victoria's age. However, she still had other 'demons' – the bullies. But this was one step closer to fighting them. Social media became a curse to her. There were many arguments we had over this. To me it didn't make sense to continue being on social media when she got such a hard time. There was no escaping it. But Victoria's point was, "Why should I leave social media because of some narrow-minded bullies?" and she had a point. When more of these bullies knew about where we lived and the stories behind our home, the teasing got worse. It seemed that once we made a breakthrough with one thing, something else happened!

Chapter XVII

Since moving away from Sharon, I always felt the urge to move back. I can't explain why, but my mother is the only other person who can relate. Considering it was only a few minutes away, it didn't feel the same. Living in the village of Newtowncunningham was lovely, but I couldn't settle there. Since Gabriel made a full recovery, I wanted to talk to him about our future and the decision on where our final home would be. I had hoped he would consider renovating one of the outhouse on the grounds of Sharon. But I knew how much work went into renovations. After discussions with my parents, we agreed to move back under the consideration that it wasn't back to the coachman's or the main building. Since the old gatehouse once graced its presence to the main entrance way, we wanted to restore it with a modern twist. I needed this to be the fresh start I had always dreamt of. I love Sharon Rectory; even with its gory past and continuous haunting, it had character. And I was now a part of its history.

When I look back over the previous 20 years, our experiences had and wavered from good, to bad, to scary, but I honestly wouldn't have changed my childhood. From the extensive renovations, to the first haunting experience, other spiritual awakenings, considering getting out, the devastation of fire, trauma, and further unworldly discoveries, from these experiences I've learned so much about myself as a person. It shaped me into the adult I am today. Some may think I'm crazy, but I know what I have experienced from a young age. I wouldn't say I'm fearless of the paranormal. It's still an unknown field of what we could face. But I feel whole, given my challenges that I tackled along the way. The gatehouse was going to be my family's future and I wasn't going to let anything stop me from living a happy life on the property of Sharon Rectory.

Summer of 2017, we finally moved in. We still had a lot of work to do, but it was comfortable to live in. Even though it was on Sharon's property, it felt different. There was no heavy energy or malevolent spirits. When renovating, I had placed blessed medals around the four corners of the building. I wanted to make sure whatever negativity lurked on the land, stayed outside. I knew it would attempt to follow me. I still could feel spirits around, but they didn't feel as engrossed as they did in the main building. It was something I was aware of when committing to move back but they didn't bother me. Now I knew what evil I could face the other spirits didn't seem frightening.

It wasn't long before Gabriel started to travel for work again. At first, I didn't feel scared in the gatehouse when he left. It was only outside I felt fear. As soon as night falls, it's pitch dark. There is no contamination from streetlights, or vehicles, it's completely isolated among trees. Gabriel leaving for work was going to be a regular thing, so I needed to put it to the back of my mind and carry on living my life in my new home with my family.

At the beginning of November, a couple of nights after Gabriel left, I felt somewhat uneasy in the house. I wouldn't say it was from something adverse, but I felt as though there was something other than me and the boys there. As I carried on doing my usual routine, I got the boys ready for bed and sat down with them before they went to sleep. Without warning, all the smoke alarms in the house triggered. I jumped up and went into each room looking to see what was causing them to switch on. I couldn't find anything. I worried in case something that wasn't visible to me was on fire. Flashbacks of the blaze years previous started to come back to me. I got a tea towel and waved it below one of the alarms to try put it off. Once they stopped, I looked around and checked in and under everything. But there was nothing to indicate why they would trigger. I calmed myself before putting the boys to bed.

As I sat down to watch TV, I couldn't help but think to myself, *What if these alarms go off when I'm in bed sleeping?* I pushed it to the back of my mind and didn't think any more of it. I went to bed after 11pm. I struggled to sleep. I couldn't help but think that something 'else' was in the room with me. I had a dim plug light placed in the corner of the room, so I wasn't in complete darkness. I still feared what lurked among the shadows, even though I was no longer in the coachman's or the main building. I rolled over and tried to fall asleep.

I woke around 1.30am to the smoke alarms going off again. I panicked. There had to have been a fire smouldering somewhere, I thought. I worried that the noise would scare the boys and tried to get them to turn off. I got the tea towel like I had done before and waved it under the alarm. But nothing. It didn't work. All the alarms continued to roar through the house. I opened the windows and doors to try to cause a draft. I didn't know what else to do. I had tried everything, but nothing seemed to work. I even pressed the reset button, but it didn't work. I rang Mum. Luckily my dad was home; I had hoped he could come over to take a look at them. Within a few minutes Dad came over, and as soon as he opened the front door, all the alarms switched themselves off. I couldn't believe it. I had spent about 20 minutes running hectically around the house trying everything to turn them off. I couldn't explain it. Dad knew I was shook up and worried. After checking the house, we couldn't find an explanation as to why they would come on. We couldn't link to anything paranormal, but I had found it very strange how this was the first time since moving into the gatehouse that I felt a spiritual presence, then suddenly alarms start to mysteriously trigger. It was how Mum described when the smoke alarms went off in Sharon. She felt that something was toying with her in the house, trying to scare her. I too started to feel that something was trying to mess with me.

It felt unnerved for a few nights after. I didn't want to fall back into the habit of being scared in my own home. This was supposed to be a fresh start. I needed to face up to whatever was scaring with me. I started to burn sage throughout the house regularly. I opened the windows and doors and went around every corner of the rooms with the burning sage. I didn't mind the pleasant spirits; I would often see them out the corner of my eye passing but when things tried to scare me or the kids, that's when it bothered me.

One dark Thursday evening, as I lifted the boys from Mum's after work, I drove down the back laneway to the gatehouse. As I pulled up to front of the house Noah began to shout at me. I stopped the car and said, "What's wrong?" He continued to tell me that I had ran over a 'man' that was in the middle of the driveway. But of course, I didn't see anyone. I asked him what he saw. He told me it was a tall man wearing a hat and black coat. This to me sounded like the same spirit man I had seen as a child. It bothered me slightly. Even though this spirit meant no harm, I felt nervous for the boys. Noah was now at the age where he questioned things. He continued to ask where the man went. To be honest it did scare me. We still had to get out of the car in complete darkness to get into the house. I knew Noah must have seen something. He was genuinely worried that I had run over someone. I got out of the car and opened the front door. When the boys went inside, I shone a torch that I kept in my car up the driveway. I didn't see anyone. But I felt someone was watching me from afar.

As the weeks passed, I still felt a presence, like I was being watched as I walked outside. My parents and Victoria continued to have unsettling things happen. Nightmares became a regular thing for all of us. December continued to be a very active time in Sharon. Christmas night 2017, while everyone was asleep, they woke to something very disturbing. Around 3am, my parents woke to the house shaking. Yes, the whole house had shook. As it happened, their bed, the lockers, the wardrobes, everything started to shake uncontrollably. It lasted for a few seconds before completely stopping. But nothing was knocked out of place. All the years we lived in Sharon we never experienced an earthquake. On Boxing Day, when Dad was telling myself and Gabriel about waking up to what seemed to be an earthquake, we looked at him, confused. "Earthquake?" I said. "We didn't experience any shaking during the night." Considering we were on the same property, it was strange. I checked the news just to see if there was an earthquake recorded, but nothing was reported. Mum seemed worried. They couldn't explain it. IF this was something 'paranormal', it had to have been a very big energy.

Later that night, as Mum went to bed, Dad remained in the kitchen watching TV. As he walked towards the kettle, he suddenly felt uneasy. This was stronger than he had ever experienced before. It was like he walked directly into something evil. He felt this presence creep over him. Dad, being a fearless man considering all that he had been through, for the first time in a long time, felt scared. He knew this was the sort of sinister 'being' that would physically cause harm. He knew right then that this was the 'thing' that caused the upheaval within the house, the constant years of bad luck, the feeling of being watched, the strange and unexplainable noises, the physical and psychological disturbances, the list went on. What I always knew was in the house, was becoming clearer.

Summer that year, Victoria decided she wanted to move into the coachman's. This wasn't taken lightly, but she reassured us that whatever resided in there, wouldn't affect her. She was confident she was able to handle it, but I had my doubts. I knew what it was capable of. It was clear that something evil was present here, and I didn't think it wise. When Mum told me that Victoria had made the decision to move, I said, "I'll give her a week." I think Victoria was already being affected by this sinister spirit and moving into an active part of the building made me very nervous. This was something intelligent and I had a feeling it may have been influencing her to move away from the main house. This sudden boost of confidence wasn't normal for Victoria. And I get that she wanted her own space, but I was shocked at how she went from being scared to walk around the house, to moving into the eeriest part of building. Victoria was already in a dark place mentally with the bullies and trolls who constantly taunted her; I knew this could feed off that emotion and become stronger.

The weekend had come for Victoria to switch rooms. Mum wanted her to try sleeping in the coachman's for a couple of nights before moving all her things. I think she too had doubts that Victoria wouldn't stay long. But she surprised us. The first week she felt fine sleeping in the dreaded room. Maybe she did have control of this. During my first few nights in the coachman's it was unbearable. The feeling of a presence constantly watching you, the noises, the shadows, it was just an unpleasant feeling. Meanwhile Victoria hadn't yet experienced any of this. *Maybe this entity had moved from within the coachman's?* I thought. Victoria had proven me wrong. Both she and Mum decided it was time for her to officially move to the coachman's. It felt more like Victoria's space once she did. She had it looking so well. She put her own stamp on it. The look of the room almost made the heaviness disappear. But it wasn't long before Victoria became uneasy. This entity was one step ahead. It was as though it made Victoria feel comfortable before creeping slowly in without her recollection.

One evening as Victoria went for a shower, she felt a burning sensation along her back. Not reading too much into it, she got out of the shower to get dried and she looked in the mirror to see if she could see why her back felt sore. She noticed three large claw marks. Of course, this completely took Victoria back. She remembered how I used to receive the same marks when living in there. The next day when I found out, I knew straight away that this caused by the entity. This was the evil that lived among us. This was its way of mocking the holy trinity. I told Victoria that she needed to move out of there as soon as possible and back into her old bedroom. For the first time, she actually listened to me. I think this was the validation she needed that she didn't have control over this. How can you control or handle something that isn't visible to the naked eye? You could feel its presence back in the coachman's, but it wasn't only restricted to here. It began to move throughout the house. I think it was controlling us more than we thought.

Even after Victoria's previous experiences, she felt the pull to go back into the coachman's. She wanted this entity to know she wouldn't fear it, but I didn't want her challenging it head on. I knew she was at risk of oppression, just like I was when in there. I became overwhelmed by the darkness and I couldn't see a way out. This was beyond our control. But Victoria decided she wanted to give the coachman's another try before moving her things back into her old room. The unexplainable scratches remained in the back of her mind. I suppose she now realised what it was capable of. She remained aware.

Mid-September she moved back to the coachman's; she struggled with controlling her fear. She would pull the bed covers over her head, praying for morning to come. Late one Thursday night, she woke to a coldness around her feet. She began to feel a pressure around her ankle, like something was trying to grab hold of her. Suddenly she felt a pull on her leg that forced her from the bed. She screamed as she hit the floor. Jumping up, she leaped into the bed, contemplating what had happened. She was scared to move. She looked around the room but still felt something in there with her. This was the most terrifying experienced she encountered. Not waiting to find out what would happen next, she ran out of the door, across the arch bedroom and into her old room. Her heart was beating rapidly. She worried in case IT followed her. When waking up Mum, she told her what had happened moments before. They both lay there scared to fall back to sleep. Because Dad was away for work, it was only them remained in the house. Would it come after them both when they were together? They sat up the remaining hours that night. I woke the next morning to messages from Victoria explaining what happened. I was shocked. I started to see my life play out like a horror movie. I knew the physical marks were possible because I encountered them, but I didn't imagine something so terrifying would happen. This was now getting out of control.

Chapter XVIII

Insomnia became a common occurrence; the long, sleepless nights were adding up. As we told a few friends what was happening, the common response was, "How can you continue to live there?" Mum still wasn't going to be scared out of her home and neither was I. We had worked hard making Sharon our home. The evil that resided with us, was going to lose. Even though this entity made itself known in the coachman's, I felt It didn't always reside here. It went somewhere else in the house. I had a feeling it may have been the cellar. It is the one place in the house I wouldn't venture alone. There were a few occasions where we heard the growls and groans from within, and with previous experiences with our mediumship group and the paranormal investigators, all the signs pointed to here. Because of all the unexplainable things to occur through the years, I devoted my spare time to researching everything paranormal. I scrolled through many articles and books, trying to find answers as to why this entity was here. I had said to Mum, "What if we contacted another paranormal group, just to see if we could get more answers?" There was still so much left to uncover and maybe the only way was to invite professionals in with equipment to get advice.

November 2018, I contacted a group from Belfast. They seemed to respond quickly when I reached out. Saturday the 24th of November, they came prepped for their investigation. We introduced ourselves and gave them a tour of the house. One of the members was a psychic medium and I was intrigued to see what he would feel. I think he felt an instant impression of evil as soon as he entered the house. He didn't want to know anything about the property or its history. He simply wanted to see what he would be able to pick up. Each room where we felt and had our most disturbing experiences, he felt unwell or uneasy in. Everything we knew that we had confirmed by documents or other people, he was able to pick up. This was amazing. It was off to a good start. Each device or piece of equipment they had, worked without hesitation. I think they were taken aback as to how easily the spirits seemed to manipulate them, and on request. The night had gone better than we first anticipated. They were such a lovely bunch of people and had confirmed a lot for us. They were keen to get back for another investigation. Maybe through more of these inquiries, we could finally find out how to gain full control of our home.

On the 1st of January 2019, I decided to tell my story to the world. I was nervous how people would react or what they would say, but I felt I was more hardened to the criticism that I would probably face. I got used to ignorant comments and judgmental slurs, but there were so many people who were genuinely interested in hearing my story. This way I was able to tell my truth and put a few yarns that were previously out there, right. I started social media pages to openly talk about what we experienced in our home and because Sharon Rectory's history was already well known, it wasn't long before people started to follow. I was shocked at the positive response I got. People even started to reach out to me about their own experiences with the paranormal. I was happy I could ease some people's beliefs and doubts that they had hidden from others. They knew I wouldn't judge or condemn them for what they experienced. I felt it was a sign that it was the right time for people to hear about our on-going horror story in Sharon. There was always that small group of people who tried to bring my story down and tear it apart, but they didn't matter. What mattered was those who followed and the people that reached out to me that I knew were true believers. If my story could help others openly talk about something that was viewed unorthodox, my own achievement was met. Why should people hide behind others' unkind comments because they have experienced something out of the ordinary? I knew what negative and unpleasant energies were out there and what they were capable of. No-one should ever experience mental or physical taunting by an entity and be scared to seek help. I understand it can make you seem crazy or doubt everything you believe in, but there are people with the same experiences that have got through the other side.

Soon, other paranormal groups got in touch, keen to investigate Sharon. We didn't know how we felt about many groups coming because we weren't sure how it would affect us while living there. I didn't want it to stir the activity, but I was curious what other groups would pick up. Every team that got in touch with me, we made sure had knowledge and experience in the field. We allowed them to investigate under the exception that we were present throughout the night. We forbade any Ouija boards to be brought onto the property. I knew how destructive these were and bringing one into Sharon now, would only ever end badly. I got to realise through study that intention is everything when communicating with spirits. If you intend to only ever communicate with the bad, well that is what would come through. We knew there was evil in the house and we didn't want it antagonised. We asked each team to remain respectful and remember that this was our home. They all were great teams and very professional. Some got more activity and evidence than others, but each had memorable nights.

One team which we seemed to connect the most was a group of people from Dublin, Paranormal Investigators Ireland. They were a close family unit and had a great energy surrounding them. Their first encounter with Sharon, was going to be with them for a very long time. When they got in touch with us, they seemed intrigued by my stories on social media and wanted to experience the house for themselves. I don't think they ever expected the house to be so alive. Like others, we arranged for their investigation for a Saturday and on the 16th of February, they came to Sharon to check out the property. We started off with the general walkthrough, an introduction to each room along with the history and our experiences that happened along the way. As we walked through the house this dull darkness lay upon each room. Given that it was gone half two in the afternoon, it felt like it was late evening. Every room felt different. The energies from one side of the building to the other felt like two separate houses. An oppressive feeling lingered between the coachman's and the back staircase. While in the main living area it felt quiet. But almost too quiet.

We began the investigation within the cellar. One by one each member of the team bravely ventured down the cellar corridor, curious as to what lay ahead. After each person described a solid black figure move in and out from the wall, we decided to investigate this 'dark figure' further. As we sat in complete darkness in the lower part of the cellar, we could sense something among us. I could see flickering orbs with the naked eye which were also caught on camera. I felt that this entity was sitting back watching us, waiting for its moment to pounce, as something else scuttered between us. As time seemed to move quickly in the cellar, there was still so much the team wanted to see. We made way to the coachman's to conduct a spirit box session. When walking into the flat I got shivers as soon as I crossed the threshold. I felt IT had followed us from the cellar. When the spirit box was on, names came through that were relevant to us. It confirmed previous spirit box sessions from other investigations which I thought was impressive given that it was a different device.

My name came up quite a lot with the questions of, "Why are you here? And what do you want?"

The response being, "Emma." It was unnerving. This dark entity had taunted me for years while I lived in the coachman's and by the sound of things, it wasn't finished.

The questions had then suggested we go upstairs

to the arch bedroom. We felt a very heavy energy within here. Many different mediums throughout the years picked up on a wiccan that once lived within Sharon, possibly dating back to the 1800s. This room was known to be 'her' room. This was something I could never get the evidence to prove, although I can't say she didn't live here. The team decided for us to sit in a circle on the floor. While standing, everyone felt like we were swaying on the spot. It felt like we were on a ship. The floor pulsed with an unknown vibration, as we had the feeling of being watched. Again, something was moving among us. It made us feel very uneasy. It was only a couple of hours in and they had already received so much validation that there was something they could not explain here.

The dining room was the room that seemed to get me in recent years. Mum always has this room looking like a museum. It is how I would imagine it would have been in the late 1800s. Every time I passed the dining room door, I would catch a glimpse of figures moving within the room, even when no-one was there. There was definitely residual energy. I suggested we sit around the table quietly for a moment, to see if we could hear anything from anywhere else in the house. It wasn't long before we started to hear strange noises. It was like footsteps from afar. Mum was at the head of the table and I could see at the corner of my eye her eyes glaze over.

I knew she was being affected by a spirit.

Darren, one of the investigators, called out for 'William', meaning Rev Hamilton. Mum turned directly to him with this gazed look upon her face, eyes almost black in colour and shouted, "Do not call me William, I am Mr Rev Hamilton, do not antagonise me." I was taken aback. The sound of her voice deepened as she spoke. I was worried for Mum; I didn't know if she had total control of this, or if it was even Rev Hamilton that was speaking through her. I asked Mr Hamilton to take a step back and tried to bring Mum back around. I debated whether or not to continue. Mr Hamilton's presence was prominent within that moment. He wasn't yet finished. As we talked among ourselves about the night of the murders, abruptly Mum banged her two fits on the table with an outburst. Everyone jumped. Hamilton had once again channelled through her and he wanted to tell his story. Mum's whole faced changed, her voice, the way she spoke, everything. She was no longer Lisa. Mr Hamilton cried out, explaining how Mrs Waller wasn't meant to be caught up within the siege that fateful night. He's carrying such guilt from his actions; he believes this should be his penance. He refuses to pass over because he was a man of the cloth and feels it's his moral duty be punished. To suffer all eternity in purgatory. He is reliving his murder over and over again. We thought it best to stop and recharge. I needed to reflect on what Mr Hamilton had said. I felt almost sorry for him, he had been made out to be this villain and bully because of his actions in life, and now he was punishing himself for his sins. This was more than I had imagined would happen. I was astonished how much this team was getting.

Although the heavy energy still remained throughout the house. This entity wasn't finished. As we ended the night's investigation in the library, the team set up the cameras and I went out to the hallway to turn off the lights. I kept feeling this uneasiness while walking down the hall, like something was going to pounce out at me. I ran into the library and sat down beside Mum and Darren. I could feel a coldness follow me into the room. There was only the light of one candle that was in the middle of the coffee table. As we listened out for further noises. Darren could see this solid black figure stand right at the threshold of the doorway into the room. Darren pointed. I could see the same thing. We were taken aback. It was right THERE, looking at us. Alex, one of the other team members started snapping pictures on his camera. But he didn't realise he has caught the exact figure me and Darren saw. When reviewing the pictures there was a mist. You could make out a face and within the outline you could see horns. My heart was in my throat. I was terrified. This had to be the entity that had taunted us over the years. This entity was masking the other spirits within the house. It wouldn't let them come through to communicate. But there it was, standing at the door waiting to be invited in. It was almost like something had stopped it from going any further. Darren became very agitated. He gazed at the doorway, saying it was 'teasing him'. He could feel something weighting him down on the spot.

When Darren got up, Alex and Nicky had to hold him back from going any closer to where the figure was standing. It was as if it was coaxing him out. Trying to take control of him. We needed to close the investigation for everyone's safety. It was becoming too dark for us, and we still needed to live here after all. While the team packed away their equipment, we noticed two red marks on each side of Alex's face. It was like something slapped him on each cheek. His eye started to turn black right there in front of us. It was like he had been punched in the eye by something unseen. This was documented by the team as soon as we observed it.

On the way home, they noticed Val's eye looking very red and bloodshot. They took a picture to show her, but she had no recollection of it happening. No-one noticed it throughout the night, so it was hard to say what exactly happened her. Val felt like it was a punishment because she refused to look at the entity standing at the library's doorway. The night was one of the most compelling we had from any other investigation. We didn't expect for as much activity to happen, but Paranormal Investigators Ireland left wanting more.

Chapter XIX

As more and more evidence from teams confirmed the haunting in Sharon Rectory, it attracted the attention of paranormal seekers far and wide. We didn't do this for fame or following. I had never expected my stories on social media to spiral overnight. We even had the local newspapers and radio stations asking us to comment on the happenings in house. I had so many people approach me, asking if they could come for an investigation. It wasn't something I had ever considered, although I knew there were so many that wanted to experience something for themselves. It was all becoming overwhelming and we still had to live with the fact these things happened every day regardless of how many groups came. We were grateful for the advice given to us by teams. It was a relief in a sense, that others were now experiencing the same events as us. But this dark entity would become more profound with each investigation. It got to the point where other spirits began to fade because it overpowered them. Rarely we would see the souls that once belonged to the house. Names of others started to come up during investigations and we couldn't seem to connect or figure out who they were. It was starting to confuse me. We had made such good progress with everything we'd got so far. I felt as though this negative one took control. IT played us, each time it made itself known. It was intelligent. It lured us into thinking it was something it wasn't. I started to catch on to it, and I think it saw me as a threat.

We decided to take a break for a few months. There were investigations nearly every weekend and we were becoming drained living in the aftermath of it all. As teams walked away, we still remained. So, from June to August we stopped. We had stayed in touch with a lot of the groups. They would tell me about some of their personal experiences coming away from Sharon. Nightmares were a common occurrence among them all. Each person who seemed to be affected within the house left and continued to experience things in their own home. I don't think it had followed them. It was that big of an energy, it was able to affect people even when they left. I worried for people's safety. I needed to make folk aware that this was possibly something that they could experience during the investigations. It wasn't to be taken lightly.

Sharon remained active throughout our break, but Mum, Victoria and I needed to escape from the activity. We decided to go away for a week. Things were unbearable in Sharon and we hadn't been on a family holiday in years. Dad and Gabriel stayed back with the kids. Since they were away the majority of the time, it was only right we too got a break from it all. I will admit, it was bliss. It was the first time in a long time I felt myself. My life with the paranormal had totally consumed me. Little did we know, Dad was experiencing something equally as terrifying as Victoria's previous year's incident in the coachman's.

On the week we were away, Dad woke on the Monday night with a strange clicking noise at the bottom of his bed. He sat up to listen for a moment, just to see where it was coming from. He was confused because he had never heard anything like it before in the room. When he sat at the edge of bed ready to get up, he felt a force pushing him back, holding him down onto the bed. He lay there frozen, like something was stopping him from moving. When whatever had hold of him released, he jumped up and opened the bedroom window. He shouted, "I do not tolerate bullies, now get the fuck out of my house." This was something he least expected in his own home. He knew this entity needed to go. It was destructive, unruly and dangerous. When he closed the window, he got back into bed; the loudest bang vibrated through the house from downstairs. He didn't even acknowledge it. This thing wanted attention and it became angry at the fact that my father stood up to it.

After our holiday, Dad sat down Victoria and Mum and proceed to tell them about what he encountered. It was a shock but wasn't surprising considering all that we had happen before. This was the final straw. We needed to get to the bottom of this entity. I knew from research that this wasn't going to leave without a fight. We needed to get its name. This was going to be difficult. Why would this 'thing' give us a name if it knew we were trying to banish it? It was going to be a very intense run, but we needed to continue this to get to the bottom of it. It wasn't as easy as getting a priest in and performing an exorcism. We needed more proof of this entity's existence. Even though we already got a lot from previous investigations, it wasn't enough. This was clever. It knew to hide from the right people. There were a few individuals from the teams that left the house deeply affected. Anyone who was supposed to help with this entity, something had stopped them from visiting the house. We saw it as a sign. This was going to be a fight. I was starting to lose hope. Nights were becoming unbearable. Even though I wasn't in the main house, things seemed to creep into the gatehouse. Gabriel was still oblivious to it all and even when I tried to talk to him about it, it caused arguments. I felt that this entity was going to win. I feared what came next.

One night, I woke with the uneasiness I felt when something in the shadows lurked near. I turned in the bed to face the window and unexpectedly, I saw a face come through my blind from the window. It peered directly at me. It was expressionless. There were no apparent features. I didn't know what it was. It appeared for a split second before disappearing. This was becoming a common occurrence.

A few months before, when I got into bed, I lay on my stomach to fall asleep. After a few minutes, I could feel pressure on the bottom of my back and below my neck. It was like something was trying to push me into the bed. I struggled to get my hand up to reach for my rosary which was beside me. When I turned my head, I could see a shadow about shoulder height, coming out from the wall. I could see the head, shoulders and body. I prayed to Archangel Michael for it to leave and within a split second it was gone. I grabbed my rosary and clutched them tightly in my hand. The next morning, I saged the whole house.

These encounters at night continued. Different apparitions were seen regularly, but I think they were all connected to this one entity. It was trying to lure us in, making us believe it was a pleasant spirit, so it could be invited in. I had to tell Mum and especially Victoria, to be careful when seeing this apparitions. The young girl that was seen frequently over the years worried me. However, we knew this spirit girl did exist; it wasn't always the actual spirit of the little girl that we were experiencing. I knew the difference because when this entity was near, I would get uncontrollable heart palpitations. It wasn't any medical issue or anxiety. This was my body's way of telling me that IT was close by. At this stage I was worried of possession. I knew we all suffered with an oppression over the years, I knew possession came next.

Since Paranormal Investigators Ireland was a team that always got great evidence in Sharon, I had hoped they could help with banishing this evil one. They knew this was no average haunting. They came face to face with this entity in the past and knew how powerful it was. Each of them experienced things that only we could relate to. With other teams still commencing investigations, we arranged that PII would come on the 2nd of November for All Souls night. On the weeks leading up, the house was alive. Victoria was having very vivid dreams that involved a strange creature. She dreamt of this reptilian being coming up from the swap land below the Glebe of Sharon. It crawled up from the dirt and reached out for her as she watched it. Many children followed it as they crept up from the marshy ground. Victoria described it as though it had reptilian skin, with straggly dark hair and razor-sharp teeth. It was something completely out of nightmares. She began to run in her dream as this creature followed her. She woke up screaming as she shot up in the bed to look around her. *Was this the entity within the house?* she thought.

She explained to me the details of her dream. "It had webbed hands and claws inches long. It reached out its claws for me, as I ran from it." She drew exactly what she saw. I took the picture and began to research into what this thing could be. I don't know if it was because I had read so many articles on demonic entities and reptilians, or if my mind was playing tricks on me, but as I fell asleep the next night, I dreamt of something very similar. In my dream, I was walking towards the back laneway beside the gatehouse. I could see something unusual standing behind one of the trees. As I focused in on it, I could see these razor-sharp claws grasp around the trunk of one of the trees. This creature looked around and I could see pointed ears and messy dark hair that creeped around its face. Then I woke. I doubted myself, thinking I had read too much into demonic presences to even believe it was real.

On the weeks leading up to Halloween, I had read that the veil between the spiritual world and physical world would be at its thinnest. Because we experienced on-going events, this didn't surprise me. We had a few investigations coming up and we were intrigued to see what we would capture. In the past we got great responses vocally by things unseen. Mum and I would always hear, "Mama," during the day when we were in the house, or a mumbling conversation from afar. In some investigations we got the same. Everything from a voice coming out of nowhere saying, "Who are you?" to someone shouting, "Hello!" We had captured some great vocal evidence.

There was a feeling in my gut about this Halloween. I had talked to Mum and Victoria about a build-up of something we might not be able to control. This doubtful feeling continued over a few days. I don't know if it was that this entity was getting into my head, or if it knew its time was coming close. Again, I felt like it was all becoming too much for me to control. Either way I had an awful feeling about it.

One Tuesday evening, Gabriel was working abroad. I was sitting down to watch TV when Jonah, my youngest son, noticed a man outside the living room window. I paused for a moment because I was scared to look out. When I turned my head to look out of the window, I didn't see anyone. It was a relief. I asked Jonah what he saw; he described this 'man' as having 'sharp teeth and big long nails'. I didn't know what to say. I knew straight away what it was. Jonah was oblivious as to what was going on and I knew no-one would have told him about what Victoria had seen. He went on to tell me, "This man was jumping up and down to look in the window and he was scratching the window to get in." I was scared to move. I didn't know what to say. Usually I would reassure the kids when they told me anything strange that they saw, but I had no words for Jonah then. I brushed it off and changed the subject, distracting him from the image that remained in his head. Thankfully he didn't mention it again after that. I couldn't help but think these were the same similarities Victoria and I witnessed in our dreams. I didn't want to think on it too much because I still had to remain alone with the kids when Gabriel worked away.

Paranormal Investigators Ireland were so excited to get back for All Souls. This was an event that only a few selected public would attend. A couple nights before, on Halloween night, Carrickfergus Paranormal Researchers got some great experiences. Both good and bad. Victoria was affected badly during this investigation. She felt extremely sick from whatever energy that surrounded us that night. I think this was a warning of what would come. As we prepared for the next investigation, I talked to Mum about continuing these events. It was taking a toll on us all. The investigations had consumed my life and every day I felt my health was deteriorating. My fibromyalgia was flaring for short periods, then easing in between. There was a feeling surrounding me that I couldn't explain. I felt that something big was yet to happen. It was going to be something that was going to shock us all. As the team got set up, I did the usual walkthrough of the house, explaining the history and our experiences to the guests that came. Kate, of course, needed to be here. I felt somewhat safe when she was near. I had someone there that I trusted and was able to help control things.

We started the investigation in the library. After a few minutes, Kate could feel a very strong energy come into the room. She described it as very large dark presence. It walked among us as it sized us out. Mum, Victoria and I, sat at the corner of the room. It's weird, because it was the corner I had always imagined Mrs Waller hid in, shielding her husband from the gunshots during that horrid night. We could feel something get closer to us. My hairs stood on edge. I felt IT right next to me. I placed a torch on top of the library books and asked it to turn it on. Without hesitation, the torch lit up. Everyone was amazed.

Something seemed to distract us throughout the night. We felt something steered us off course when something was about to happen. We moved into the sitting room because noises seemed to come from the hallway between both rooms. Maybe it would interact better with us in the sitting room. I sat on the far window ledge opposite the doorway to the patio hallway. I could see the end of the staircase. I felt disconnected from the group. I couldn't zone into what was going on. It was like something was pulling me away from everyone. Every time we felt we were getting somewhere, there were strange lights shining out in the street. But when we went to check, there was no-one. It pulled us away from the investigation. I was agitated. There was an anger building up inside me that I couldn't control. I felt like I was going to combust. I never told anyone because I wasn't sure of this emotion. It didn't feel like it was mine. I was being manipulated by something that was around me. I tried to shake it off and when moving out to the staircase, I felt it ease. It was as if the aim was off me and onto someone else. Elaine, from the team, stood at the top of the staircase and faced the mirror. She became very unsteady and within seconds, she fell to the floor. I knew then this entity was targeting her. She was very defocused for the rest of the night. After a short time, I suggested a break. Things were becoming extremely intense. I didn't like it. I could feel the rage building inside me yet again, and I didn't know where it was coming from.

During a short break I went outside to one of the outhouses to light candles to cast some light for when we moved outside. I needed the fresh air. I was becoming overwhelmed. I didn't know how to control these emotions that weren't mine. I had never channelled a spirit before, I felt like this may have been the start of something trying to control me. When I was in the outhouse, I heard shuffling and movement from the room next door. I peered through the doorway, but I couldn't see anything. I was scared; I had a feeling this entity was near. I could feel my heart beating as I ran into the house. I asked Mum and Victoria to come with me outside. I didn't want to admit to the others I was frightened. But this thing was taunting me. It was surrounding me throughout the night, and I couldn't deal with it. I felt I was suffocating. As soon as we stepped outside into the courtyard, I saw two glowing white eyes peering out of the corner outhouse. I shouted to Mum and Victoria, but it was gone before they could even see it. I think it followed the three of us. I think it knew what lay ahead.

Kate suggested investigating the dining room. A few of us sat around the table while Kate and the others observed. There was a guest who I was extremely impressed with. He studied the rite of exorcism along with Latin and had a very strong presence about him. He had a solid authority and I had hoped he would be the one to identify this evil one. As he observed quietly throughout the night, he studied the events as they occurred. When we sat around the table I sat next to Mum, with Darren sat at the opposite side. Dave stepped forward. He began to recite a prayer in Latin. Mum all of a sudden started to exhale uncontrollably. Her face was the site of worry. We knew Mum started to feel the fret of this entity. I had my hand placed on Mum's and I started to feel her pull away from mine. I gripped her tightly, telling her to fight the thoughts of this entity. I called upon Archangel Michael because I knew this wasn't going to end well.

As Dave continued prayer in Latin, this entity completely took hold of Mum. She began to laugh uncontrollably and started talking in tongues. Me and Victoria looked at each other because we knew this was risky, letting her continue. Dave resumed and demanded it to give us a name. It laughed through Mum and mocked him as he persisted with the prayers. I felt like I was in a daze. Everything around me didn't feel real. I looked over at Dave and I could feel my eyes glaze over. My head was so dizzy. I could feel myself blacking out. Thankfully, Darren called Kate to help me. I couldn't speak to shout for help. I was aided out of the room by Kate. This was the strongest I have ever left this entity. It takes a lot for me to leave an investigation because I consider myself a strong person spiritually. Even though I went through terrifying ordeals in the house, I rarely ran.

When Kate helped me into the kitchen, I felt like I was burning up. My body was boiling from the inside out. I remember describing to Kate, "I feel like I'm burning in hell." She could feel my body burning through my layers of clothes. I knew I was under an oppression. We could hear Mum laugh as she shouted out, "That's one down." Kate ran back into the dining room. With the help from another guest, I started to come around. I could hear them making leeway in the dining room. I needed to observe as they continued. This was the evidence we needed to help us banish this from the property.

Dave continued to recite prayers and asked questions. I wasn't sure if Mum was capable of channelling this entity for a long period. I didn't want it to affect her long-term once she welcomed it into her. She talked in a different language. I knew she didn't know the phrases she was speaking. Dave was able to translate some sentences such as, "Hello," and, "You are my servants." As the tension built up, I walked closer into Mum's view. I could see her face physically change into what I can only describe as an old hag. Darren asked Dave to continue with prayers. We could see Mum becoming extremely agitated. Her head peeked between her shoulders and torso. She almost looked distorted. This wasn't her. I looked over at Kate. We were worried she may have been overcome by this entity. As soon as Dave began the casting out prayer, Mum let the loudest and fiercest roar from the pit of her stomach. I ran to her and held the cross of my rosary on top of her head. Kate grasped her hand and we both began to pray. Dave continued to recite prayers in Latin and me and Kate called forth the Archangels. Mum screamed uncontrollably. She was fighting whatever was inside her. I could feel the sweat beating off her. She was completely overcome by this dark one. For a moment I thought we lost her.

Dave continued to cast of this evil one from Mum. We could see a release within her. Her body which was so tense before, eased back into the chair. She started to come around. She could still feel 'it' still in her hands; she told us not to let her go. Dave ended with a blessing and 'it' released its hold on Mum. I called the investigation. I couldn't risk Mum going through that again. It was something I never wanted to witness again. It was confirmed we were dealing with a demon and a very powerful one at that. I knew for so long that this presence I felt belonged in Hell. Dave told us he could feel seven personalities from this one beast. This started to make sense. It would explain all the 'spirits' we encountered throughout the years that we couldn't connect with the house. I felt that demon was mimicking 'others' to lure us in. To give us a false sense of security, making us think we only had lost souls, looking for help. I was deeply disturbed by what went on.

When we rounded everyone up after the investigation, I felt like I had been hit by a train. My body was weak. I couldn't concentrate when someone talked to me. Dave said this demon was on the grounds long before the house was built. The darkness of Sharon's history enticed it as the horrid events unfolded. It fed off the deaths, fear, and anger. It was getting its consistent supply from our fear while we remained in the house. Every shadow, every growl we heard, even when our hearts raced, it fed off all these emotions. This was much worse than we first anticipated. Dave strongly advised us not to let Mum under the oppression of this demon again. This was strong enough to kill. I knew people would never believe what had happened. It was sensitive in nature and I didn't want to face the condemnation from others. I was really scared for my family. This demon may have been weakened, but it wasn't banished.

The aftermath of All Souls Night was no better. It was tormenting us more than ever. We struggled to sleep at night. Even members from PII and the public were facing awful nightmares. I lay wake most of the nights reliving Mum's screams. The knocks and bangs continued in Sharon as well as the gatehouse. We believe it went away to build up energy before returning once again to taunt us.

Dad had been away for more than a month and I worried for Mum and Victoria in the house on their own. Victoria was experiencing extreme insomnia. She never closed an eye. The only time she got any sleep was when she lay on the couch during the day for a quick nap, and I was the same. Mum continued to wake every night at 1:05am. There was no specific reason why, but it reoccurred night after night. The following Tuesday, Victoria woke to the sound of Mum breathing frantically. It sounded like she was channelling through a spirit while she slept. Victoria jumped from the bed and ran into the room. Mum turned her head and opened her eyes. She asked if she was okay. Mum continued to node her head with a yes. Victoria wasn't convinced. She continued to walk through the bedroom to use the bathroom and when looking back, she noticed a dark shadow scamper across the floor of the room. When Victoria told me about Mum's strange response, I worried in case the demon was taking possession. She had no recollection of breathing erratically during the night. I contacted Darren from PII who was currently seeking help from an external force. We waited for the phone call, but the days seemed to pass. I had guidance from other folk for means of protection and other ways to help ease the energy within the house. It was all much appreciated, but it only ever eased things for a short time. We all wore blessed St. Benedict and St. Michael's medals and I always kept my rosaries with me.

It was coming to a week after the investigation, we still didn't sleep through the night. I felt like I walked around like a zombie. I was zapped of all my energy. I knew myself I was giving into it, letting it wear me down. I had cancelled any teams that were due to investigate over the coming weeks. I knew it would run the risk of it all happening again. When going into Sharon I carried my rosaries and other forms of holy protection with me. I had stopped the boys from going into the house. I didn't want to expose them directly to where it seemed the strongest. When entering into the house, anytime I placed my rosary beads around my neck, I felt them burn. It was like they were dipped in boiling hot water, then positioned around my neck. I felt that this demon was trying to strip me from all holy elements. It wasn't long before Victoria felt the same thing with her rosary.

As the days passed, we still hadn't heard anything from the help we were evidently getting from the clergy. The presence from this demon lingered and could be seen scuttling in the house. On the Saturday following the investigation, when Mum finally fell asleep, she woke to her chain with a St. Benedict medal choking her. She struggled as she pulled the chain loose from around her neck. She wasn't going to let it engage her. With the strong faith in her angels she called upon them to help. She felt it leave from around her.

The days passed and we still hadn't heard anything from the people who were supposed to help. On the Thursday night, I woke screaming with something crawling on me in the bed. I could feel a heaviness on my legs like something was sitting on me. When I opened my eyes, I couldn't see anything. Thankfully Gabriel was with me. He shot up and looked around the room but couldn't see anything. I just lay there and cried, wondering when was this all going to end. I didn't know if it was getting into my head or if it was now creeping into my house to torture me. It seemed to make the attacks at night, when we were most vulnerable. I felt as though it weakened us as we were gearing up for the flight to banish it. Maybe the demon was keeping the people that was coming to help away. It had happened before, what's to say it wasn't happening again?

Victoria started to beg her boyfriend or friends to stay overnight. She was waking to a dark shadow sitting in the chair opposite her bed, watching her as she slept. She continues to see the shadow nightly sitting in the chair watching her.

It's been three weeks since the investigation. We are still undertaken by this demon and its oppressive torture. We know it continues to use our fears against us and wear us down by affecting our sleep. As I sit here and write about the current phenomena, I don't know when it's going to end. Help seems to be coming, but without validation, I can't see the light at the end of the tunnel just yet. I fear the worst is yet to come. I am afraid this entity is going to tear my family apart. We are trying to stay positive and surround ourselves with the healing light of God. But living in constant fear of the unknown, it's hard to see a way out. As the spirits of Mrs Waller, Rev Hamilton and the others seem to fade, this nameless demon continues to overpower and doom them to remain stuck, helpless while it consumes Sharon and all within it. We hope they can return once again, as we banish this entity from the land, back to Hell for all eternity.

References

Maturin, C. *Melmoth the Wanderer*, Volume III, Oxford University Press, 1986 (p255-256).

ABOUT THE AUTHOR

Emma Louise Tully was born on December 13th, 1989 and was raised in the small village of Newtowncunningham in County Donegal, Ireland. While growing up, Emma faced unexpected challenges as she embarked on a journey with the paranormal. It all began when her parents fell in love with a dilapidated Georgian mansion. The family took on an immense project of renovation and spent most of their life savings bringing this former Church of Ireland rectory back to its former glory. When finally moving into their new home, unexplainable events began to unfold. Emma's childhood was like no other. Her ability to see and hear spirits was enhanced when residing with the ghosts from the past.

After leaving high school in 2007, she went on to study health and social care in the North West Regional College and later was employed by a private healthcare agency as a Personal Healthcare Assistant. Despite the attempts to lead a normal life, Emma's curiosity in the paranormal grew as she began her research for answers as to why her home held such activity.

Over the last year, Emma has worked alongside some of the most profound Irish paranormal groups to gain knowledge and understanding in the field of the supernatural. She has done many radio and live video interviews regarding her personal experiences living in Sharon Rectory. As the paranormal is a growing interest for many, Emma has held numerous events such as paranormal investigations and historical tours within the spectacular Georgian rectory.

You can follow her on-going story at:

www.facebook.com/SharonRectory

www.instagram.com/sharon_rectory_donegal_ireland

Printed in Poland
by Amazon Fulfillment
Poland Sp. z o.o., Wrocław

54965292R10134